STORIES FROM THE CAFÉ

VOLUME ONE

KAT SIMONS

T&D PUBLISHING

STORIES FROM
THE CAFÉ

CONTENTS

INTRODUCTION
WELCOME TO THE CAFÉ

Welcome to The Café at KatSimonsBooks!

Growing up, I loved the idea of having bookstore with a coffee shop attached. I came across one for the first time in the eighties in San Diego—this was before Barnes and Noble included a café in their stores. This was actually before Barnes and Noble—and I loved this idea so much it stuck with me for a very long time. Decades really.

But the realities of owning a physical bookstore, nonetheless a physical bookstore with a coffee shop attached, were not in the cards for me. My life took me in other directions. And while I would have loved to have just such an establishment near to me wherever I lived, those kinds of independent bookstores with coffee shops seem to be rare on the ground. At least here in the US. (I'm not sure what happened to the one in San Diego, whether it's still there or not, but I seem to recall hearing that it is not, mores the pity.)

At any rate, the idea of a bookstore-café remained a dream hovering in the back of my head for all these years.

And then I opened a virtual bookstore of a sorts. A store that is dedicated to my own fiction and merchandise and things, of course, but still. A bookstore. KatSimonsBooks. For all things I write, and that my other pseudonym, Isabo Kelly, writes. One morning, while noodling over ways to make the store a place readers would like to visit regularly, ways to make it a welcoming place to hang out, and to provide readers with something fun each time they dropped by, it hit me…

I could have a café.

A virtual one. But still. A café. Attached to my bookstore.

The idea took root, though it took me some time to figure out how to make it work. And to be honest, as I write this, it's still in the very early stages of development. *But* one of the most important things I wanted to do was to provide regular, free stories for people to read at the café, something that would give back as well as encourage people to come to the site. And I decided that all those stories should be set in "The Café."

Of course, since this is a magical café—because I get to say so—I could have characters from all my series show up in the stories, make guest appearances, cameos. Even characters who don't exist in the same story "universe." The café could have its own unique cast of regulars. And maybe sometimes all these characters might even interact at The Café. No rules because, well, magic.

So that's what I did. Built a virtual café (that is still

developing), with merchandise, and coffee (yes actually coffee for sale! Although that's in limited territories until I can source some more distributors), and stories. Lots of stories. Twice a month, a new story from the café releases and is free to read for two weeks before the next story posts.

What you have in this first collected volume of those stories are the first thirteen tales from The Café. The first story in the collection is the origin story of the café, it's owner—a witch named Nina and her familiar, a cat named Boo. From there, we meet some of the occasional patrons who pass through, some of the regulars—like Agnes and Frank and Jamar. There are standalone stories with one visit characters. There are guest appearances from Myra and Christopher, from my Dragon Thief series, Cary and Deacon, from The Cary Redmond series, and Joan from the Joan of Kerry series. And there's a second story from Nina's perspective again, as we learn a little more about her love interest.

The first six months' worth of Stories from the Café, and the origin stories and beginnings of the café, are inside this volume.

While the individual stories are posted for free for two weeks, I also wanted to ensure readers could go back and get the stories they wanted to read. Especially since some of them, like Nina and Boo, are continuing stories. A series inside the series if you will. The STORIES FROM THE CAFÉ collections are here so readers can catch up on anything they've missed, keep a copy of the stories for themselves, and for my print readers, to have access to everything as well.

And there are more stories to come! The Café continues beyond this volume, with new stories every 1st and 15th of the month. If this is your first introduction to The Café, I encourage you to make regular visits to TheCafeatKatSimonsBooks.com for new stories and fun! I hope you find a virtual space you enjoy hanging out in, with plenty of stories both big and small to enjoy.

So grab yourself a mug of something nice to drink. Then settle in as you get to know The Café.

Welcome!

Kat Simons
June 2025

BOO AND THE WITCH
AT THE CAFÉ

OUR STORY BEGINS...

Nina straightened the mugs behind the counter for the hundredth time and gave the espresso machine a final rubdown. The wooden tables and wooden countertop sparkled, polished so smooth they looked like glass. The trays with cupcakes, croissants, and slices of sweetbread on the counter looked delicious under their glass display domes. The air was thick with the delicious scents of coffee beans and vanilla. All the silverware was clean and aligned in the tray under the counter. The milk was fresh. The sugars and sweetener packets all arranged just so. The individual packets of various teas arranged so customers could select their favorites.

The café was as ready as it was going to get.

She pulled in a deep breath, set a hand to her stomach to quiet her nerves. Then went back to aligning the white ceramic mugs just so.

"It'll be fine," Boo assured from his perch on a tall stool to one side of the cash register. His huge, hairy body sprawled over the seat that was too small for him, but he didn't seem to notice and showed no signs of having any bones anyway. A Maine coon with pale gray fur and pale blue eyes, Boo was the sort of cat that lived up to his name. Fluffy. Ghost like. And a little scary when he wanted to be.

"Opening day," Nina said. "It's supposed to be nerve-wracking. Right?"

"We're attached to a bookstore. Bookstore people love coffee shops. Coffee shop people love bookstores. It's a match made in heaven." He stretched his long body and slid off the stool, landing gracefully in a lump of fluffy gray fur on the wooden floor. After another stretch, he wandered toward the front door, which still had the Closed sign hanging in front of the glass.

On the windows bracketing the door, Nina had painted some flower designs and stenciled in the opening day menu because the windows looked bare and needed decorating. Boo hadn't argued with her, so she assumed it wasn't too ridiculous.

She straightened her white apron, with the café logo on the front, and then pulled in a deep breath and let it out slowly. "Okay. We're ready."

As she walked to the front door, she glanced through the wide, open archway between the café and the bookstore. Everything on that side of the things was perfect. The cheerful owner of the bookstore hummed as she straightened some shelves, preparing to open her own doors.

The cheerful humming and the combined smell of coffee and books filled Nina with a needed shot of dopamine. Everything was going to be fine. Great even! Like Boo said, loads of people liked books and coffee. Lots of people liked those two things combined. This was going to be fun.

"Just remember not to talk in front of the customers," she warned Boo, even as she flipped the sign and hoped for actual customers today.

"Now that's just insulting," Boo said. "Would you say that to a bodega cat?"

"Bodega cats don't talk to me and comment on my pastry choices."

"That's because they know their jobs. I do too." Boo delicately, and deliberately, licked one large, furry paw.

"Fine." Having a familiar was pretty typical for a witch, and a cat was well-nigh cliché. But Boo had been with her longer than she cared to think about. He was a trusted companion and had championed this idea of a café next to the local bookstore. So she had a lot to thank him for.

To show that thanks, she returned to the counter and got out his chunky ceramic food dish and filled it with some of his favorite soft food, setting it all well away from the food and drink prep areas. She needed her good rating to stay in business. But Boo deserved his nice breakfast.

Boo, for his part, agreed.

———

The morning went slowly, with not a soul stepping through the main entrance for the first couple of hours. The sidewalk through the front windows had decent pedestrian traffic. They were in a relatively good part of town. But it was a work day, and everyone beyond the door seemed to be in a hurry. Too much of a hurry to stop in at a random, newly opened café, where they couldn't be sure how fast their coffee would reach them.

A couple of browsers came into the bookstore in the late morning, though, and they wandered beneath the wide arch into the café, smiling and taking deep breaths, filling up on the lovely smells. Nina happily brewed them each large coffees—one in a to-go cup and one in a mug. The customer who got the coffee in the mug, sat near the window and sipped her coffee while reading one of the books she'd bought, a stack of four more sitting on the table next to her.

That was Nina's ideal moment. Sitting and reading and drinking coffee, with a comforting pile of books close to hand. *That's* what she wanted from her café, what she wanted this place to be for people.

Lunchtime brought a few more customers in from the bookstore. One of whom gave Boo a little coo and, after asking permission—of Boo, not Nina—gave the Maine coon a thorough scritch around the head and ears. Boo purred throughout and was in a fine mood after that customer took her to-go coffee and left through the front door. That was the first time the little bell over the door jingled.

Nina tried to memorize the sound. She wanted to put a little spell on the door, something that would encourage people to come inside. But at the same time, she wanted to do this without magic. Wanted this to succeed on its own merits, not because she'd lured people in with a spell. She wanted to lure them with the coffee and pastries.

The afternoon went quiet again, but as people started getting out of work, things picked up in the bookstore, and that spilled over into the café. In fact, the bell over the front door jingled twice with customers coming in off the street. That delighted Nina. She'd been starting to worry that wouldn't happen. And if she only got people in front the bookstore, well, that was great too. That was the point of her business and the bookstore being linked. But it was nice to have people come her way first.

And, of the two customers who came in through the café, one of them wandered into the bookstore after sitting and drinking their coffee for a bit. That was what Nina and the bookstore owner had hoped for! People moving between the two places. People seeing them as part of a whole.

When she was behind the counter, wiping down the espresso machine, Boo jumped up onto the stool beside the register and whispered, "Told you this would work."

She reached back and gave him a scratch around the head. Then washed her hands for the purposes of food safety and customer reassurance.

By the end of the day, she'd had about a dozen customers through the place and was feeling better than she had that morning. Not a landslide. Not a crush. But a good start to a new venture.

The bookstore owner poked her head around the open

archway between their stores. "Everything go well today?" She adjusted her glasses, her eyebrows raised in question.

"Great. I actually had customers. That was my biggest hope for opening day."

"So you're staying?"

"I'm staying."

The bookstore owner grinned and tapped the wooden post on the wall. "See you tomorrow then."

Nina was delighted to confirm she would, in fact, be back the next day.

———

Which was a lot slower than the first day. The bookstore owner assured her it was just because it was a Wednesday and by the weekend, things would pick up. Tuesdays were usually pretty good because those were new release days, which was why Nina had opened the coffee shop that day instead of Monday. She'd been warned things would be quiet and busy in waves and to expect the quiet.

Still, when she got to the end of the day and had only served two cups of coffee and sold one pastry, she was a little sad.

Boo gave her calf a gentle swat. "Buck up. It'll work out."

"I'm holding you to that."

B y the weekend, she realized she might need to hire help.

At least for the weekend. From the moment she turned the sign to Open in the café's front door at ten in the morning on Saturday, people came in and out. More even than the bookstore for the morning. She sold out of the muffins and sweetbreads she had on her stands by noon. Sold out of the cupcakes she'd ordered based on hope more than evidence by two. And by the time she turned the Open sign back to Closed that night, she was run off her feet, exhausted, and thrilled.

But she was going to need some help sooner rather than later.

"Good day!" the bookstore owner said, poking her head back around the archway again, as she did every evening when they closed up shop at the same time.

"Good day," Nina said with a grin. Boo, for his part, spent most of the day smugly purring from his stool next to the register.

M onday all the weekend activity died. Nina wasn't sure whether to be relieved or panicked.

Boo shook his head. "Are you entirely sure you're cut out for this?" he asked as he cleaned his fluffy paws and watched her fretfully watching the silent front door.

"No," she sighed. "I'm not sure I'm cut out for this. But I love the place, so I'm hopeful."

"I'm not going to repeat it'll be fine because I hate repeating myself."

"I will point out that you just did."

Boo ignored her comment completely. "But I think you should take this quiet time to decide what sort of employee you want."

"I've never hired anyone before," she admitted.

"Good time to look for help from someone who has."

Their conversation was disrupted by the front door's bell ringing. Nina straightened from her slouch on the counter and smiled at the man who walked in, trying not to look desperate or maniacal and afraid she failed miserably.

"Welcome to the café," she said. "What can I get you?"

The man returned her smile, his looking significantly more relaxed. It was a nice smile. A very nice smile. Nina blinked a few times.

A very very nice smile.

And extremely nice brown eyes.

He was probably in his early thirties, though she was a terrible judge of people's ages because she looked in her early thirties, too, and she was a little over eighty-three years old. He was clean shaven, his brown hair trimmed into a short but loose style. Dressed in a tailored suit in a dark gray color, with a tie-dyed tie in maroons and blues. The tie was in direct contrast to the rest of his more conservative uniform. She liked it.

"Coffee, please."

"To go or to stay?" Did she ask that too hopefully? She hoped she didn't ask that too hopefully.

Eighty-three years old and she still got tongue-tied around a handsome man.

"To go, I'm afraid." He nodded at his suit. "Work."

He glanced around the empty café and Nina tried not to get antsy and defensive. Yes, it was quiet. It was Monday.

When he faced her again, though, he was smiling. "Nice place. New?"

"We just opened last week."

"Great. I love the bookstore, but having a coffee shop attached is perfect."

"We thought so, too."

Boo picked that moment to stroll around the edge of the counter and walk right up to the man. He plonked down at the man's feet and stared up at him. The man looked at Boo, his grin crooked.

"Beautiful cat," he said.

"His name is Boo," she introduced just as Boo started to preen and lick his paws.

"Great name for a gray cat."

"Boo thought so."

Boo took that opportunity to rub up against the man's leg, which left a nice collection of light gray hair on the man's dark gray slacks.

Nina winced. "Sorry. Boo, stop."

"No, it's okay," the man said, chuckling.

It was a good chuckle. Deep. Relaxed. Did something that involved tingles to Nina's stomach.

"I like cats," the man said. "And dogs."

This earned a purr from Boo. Boo liked dogs, too. They

were his favorite pet. Boo didn't consider himself a pet, because familiars weren't pets.

"Animal person." Nina nodded in approval, too. "But still. Sorry about your suit." Boo only shed when he wanted to, when he was claiming a human as his own. That he was claiming this stranger sparked Nina's suspicions.

He shrugged at the cat hair. "I've got one of those handy rollers in my desk."

"What do you do?"

The man winced. "Lawyer. Sorry."

She laughed. "For what?"

"Most people's first reaction when I tell them I'm a lawyer fall into two categories. They either think I'm rich and they hate me. Or they think I'm a scumbag and they hate me. Sometimes the hate is fear instead. But mostly, those two categories."

"Oh. That's harsh. Lawyers have their place in the world. Same as bookstores and coffee shops." And witches and their cat familiars.

She could relate to people making assumptions based on one's career.

His friendly smile did that tingly thing to her stomach again.

She handed him the to-go cup of coffee, took his cash, and tried not to make sappy moon-eyes as he walked out the door with a promise to come back again.

Sighing, she leaned on the counter, propping her chin in her hand.

"You should have gotten his name," Boo said.

Damn. She should have gotten his name.

By Saturday, the handsome man hadn't returned again, which would probably have been a bit sad if Nina didn't have so many other things to do and worry about. Like the fact that things picked up pace again by the weekend and she was being run off her feet. The weekdays were slow enough so far, she could handle those. But the weekends. Especially Saturday…

She needed help. And she'd discovered over the course of the week that hiring someone was going to be complicated. Still, after some conversation with the bookstore owner, they decided Nina could simply hire one of the bookstore employees part-time. A nice young woman named Akira, who was always in the market for more hours, and she had experience working at some of the really fast-paced coffee shops in the city.

With her employee issue solved—at least the immediate one—Nina settled in to the busy Saturday, knowing she'd have help the next Saturday. The flow of traffic into and out of the café through the front door as well as the bookstore kept her behind the counter, and she ran out of most of her pastries again by the middle of the afternoon, despite ordering more. She'd have to adjust that again.

Boo wandered out among the customers a few times, and was greeted by some with friendly smiles and others indifferent nods. Boo randomly rubbed up against both sorts of greetings. No one ever got upset about that. Which was down to Boo and his purr more than the individual person's like of cats.

During a rare break, Nina looked out the front windows and tried to decide if they'd be able to get sidewalk permission for tables out there when the weather got warmer. It would be a nice addition, but also more work. She'd have to think about that. Maybe once Akira started…

As she was staring at the people passing by in front of the café, she spotted a man whose general demeanor gave her pause. He was average height, average looking, nothing that particularly stood out. Light brown hair cut short, light skin, an ordinary face, clean shaven. He was dressed for the weekend and the weather in jeans and t-shirt with a light jacket.

And he was staring at the café with an intense frown that Nina could practically feel through the windows.

Huh.

He didn't look familiar. But after more than eighty years, she sometimes forgot faces. Not too often. But it did happen. She got distracted by a customer from the bookstore coming in for a coffee, and by the time she glanced out the window again, the man was gone.

Bit strange but she supposed occasional strange looks were to be expected.

As closing time approached, the number of people in the café was surprisingly high still, with people lingering over drinks as they read their books. She enjoyed that part so much she was reluctant to warn everyone closing time was approaching. But she was exhausted. She needed to close up and go home to sleep.

A good exhausted, though. Things were going so well.

———

Monday morning the man with the great smile showed up again. Nina was all smiles herself as she greeted him. His suit today was a navy that suited his complexion, and he looked like he'd gotten a haircut during the week, because his style was a bit shorter and sharper.

"Everything going good?" he asked as she made his coffee with milk.

"So far," she said. "I had to hire someone to help at the weekends. That's a good sign, right?"

"Great news. Means people have really taken to the place." He took the cup she handed him. "And you do make a good coffee."

She grinned. "I've had a lot of practice this week."

He flashed her that wonderful smile and said, "I look forward to my next visit."

"Yeah. Me too." She watched him walk out the door, leaning on the counter, feeling all soft and warm inside.

"You forgot to get his name again," Boo said.

———

Nina noticed the woman for the first time on Tuesday. She was pretty sure the same woman had been in the coffee shop before. At least twice before. But the woman was quiet when she ordered, and then just sat in a corner with her books, and didn't draw much attention to herself. So Nina hadn't paid her any notice.

But by the time she appeared at the counter for the third time, Nina noticed her. And not just because she was a returning customer—Nina did want to make sure she knew the regulars so she could greet them personally and make sure their experience in her café was as pleasant and friendly as possible.

"The woman?" she whispered to Boo where he sat on his stool perch, licking a paw.

Nina had her back to the main seating area, washing mugs, but she didn't have to nod or even be specific which woman she was talking about with Boo. Not least because it was midday on Tuesday and there weren't a lot of people in the café. There'd be more later. Tuesdays were release days at the bookstore so there was an uptick in people at the café on those days, just as the bookstore owner had assured her. Right now, though, there were exactly two people in the café. Both were women. Still, Nina knew she didn't have to tell Boo which one.

Boo let out a short, sharp sound that was half purr, half growl. Deep in his throat. It was a cat noise, something no one would blink at, but Nina heard the words in that noise. "Noticed her too."

Nina dried and put away the mugs, but kept glancing at

the woman. She wasn't doing anything in particular. Just sitting and reading, as usual. Quiet. Not even looking around much. But there were…sparks coming off her. That was the only word Nina had for it. Sparks of electricity like static. Nina thought if she got closer to the woman, that static would make her own arm hair rise.

It was a strange sort of magic.

Not its existence per say. Nina was a witch, after all. She was used to magic. And after so many years, she'd encountered most types.

No, this was strange because it hadn't been there the last time the woman came in.

"Weird," she murmured.

Boo let out a snort and went back to licking his front paw.

"You're going to get a hairball," she commented idly, watching the woman without making it obvious she was watching the woman.

After finishing her coffee, the woman set her mug into the tray for dirty dishes that Nina had set up near the trash bins and milk station, then left without a word.

The sparkles of magic around her that hadn't been there previously left Nina with a lot to think about.

***

The woman was back on Friday. The sparks of static-like magic jumped around her again. This time stronger. She came to the counter and quietly ordered coffee, black, with a splash of milk that she got herself from the milk and sweetener station. Then she sat in her usual corner with her usual books and started reading as she sipped her drink.

The café was quiet again. Friday mid-morning. Later, Nina had learned, things would pick up a bit. Friday afternoons and evenings brought in people looking to wind down after a long week. The bookstore usually did good business. And so did Nina. But at the moment, it was quiet.

The woman didn't do anything in particular. The strange magic sent little sparks off her, but she didn't seem to even notice them. When she'd ordered her coffee this time, Nina paid close attention. But unlike her assumption, she didn't feel the magic like static. Didn't feel anything when the woman was close. She could still *see* the magic, but she couldn't feel it.

Which was unusual because Nina could normally feel magic.

"What do you think it is?" she murmured to Boo as she made a show of cleaning the counters and straightening the area behind the espresso machine, so the woman wouldn't know she was being watched.

"Protective," Boo murmured, also making a show of not watching the woman by appearing to sleep on his stool. He whispered, so the woman and the two other people in the café wouldn't hear him.

That in and of itself was strange, because Boo did know the assignment, and he never actually spoke when there were people in the café. That he'd felt compelled to say anything meant it was important.

So. Protective magic. That wasn't a bad thing. If it kept the woman safe, Nina supposed there was no reason to worry about it. Though now she was a little worried about the woman.

F riday afternoon and evening picked up, just as it had the week before, and Nina was looking forward to having a little help on Saturday. She hadn't opened the café on Sunday the last couple of weekends, but the bookstore was still open on Sundays, so she wanted the café to remain open too. If Akira turned out to be helpful, maybe they could make arrangements for Sundays.

The Friday evening crowd lingered, so a lot of people were sitting at the tables scattered around the main floor and moving in between the café and the bookstore. Which gave the place a nice, cozy vibe. Nina stayed so busy making fresh mugs of coffee and tea, she almost missed when the woman returned. That was surprising. She didn't normally come in twice in one day.

Nina smiled at her and said, "You're back."

The woman seemed startled Nina remembered her but returned her smile with a shy nod. "I love this bookstore and the coffee shop just makes it perfect. I could live here."

"Ah, I'm so glad you like it. We were hoping it would be something nice for people."

"Oh, it is. I love it. It's…" She glanced around, smiled at

Boo. When she met Nina's gaze again, she shrugged. "I don't know. It feels really safe."

Nina wasn't entirely sure what to say to that, but the woman didn't seem to expect a response. She took her coffee and the two books she'd brought over from the bookstore and went looking for a seat. She ended up sharing a table with another woman, since the place was crowded, but the two seemed to have the same idea of quietly reading, so it looked like a good fit.

The sparking magic was still surrounding the woman but closer to her body, and it didn't seem to bother the woman across from her. Nina hadn't felt it at the counter again either. Whatever it was, it hadn't seemed to bother any of the customers the woman passed.

With things so busy, Nina didn't have time to dwell on the woman and her protective magic, though, and lost track of her as the evening passed. She thought the woman had left, only to see her seated at another one of the tables in the center of the café, a new customer across from her. A much older woman this time, who was sipping tea and reading a book of erotica. Nina was having trouble remembering everyone she'd served tonight, but she remembered the older woman. She'd also been in the café a few times now. She always ordered tea, and she loved her racy books and poetry. Nina had liked her immediately.

Apparently, the younger woman's protective magic liked the older woman too, because it seemed to be sparking around her as well now. Neither woman showed any reaction to it, so Nina didn't feel the need to intervene. She was just glad the woman had something to keep her safe.

Things started to wind down in the last half hour before closing, the sidewalk outside busy with a lot of pedestrian traffic, but inside, the number of customers had dwindled to a handful between the coffee shop and the bookstore.

The woman with the protective magic remained, onto her third cup of coffee. The older woman she'd been sitting with had left about twenty minutes ago. None of the sparking magic went with her, though. That all stayed with the younger woman.

Nina went up to clear one of the used mugs off her table and smiled at her when she looked up. "I'm Nina, by the way. Since you're a regular now."

"Mandy," the woman said in return. "Nice to meet you, Nina. I like the idea of being a regular some place."

"I like the idea of having regulars! Glad you found us." She wanted to ask Mandy if she was okay but that was intrusive and really none of her business.

Her business was making sure the dishes were cleaned and the cash register emptied and the bank deposits readied. Her business was ensuring the café could open tomorrow morning. So she went back to that. But she did worry a little about Mandy.

Saturday turned out to be a bright, sunny day, and that seemed to bring out even more people to the bookstore. All those people flowed into and out of the café, which made Nina extremely grateful that it was Akira's starting day and she knew exactly what she was doing. In fact, she knew how to run the espresso machine and served customers more efficiently than Nina did.

Nina was going to have to buy the bookstore owner a present or flowers or chocolate or something as thank you for introducing her to Akira.

By noon, the tables were full, the traffic between bookstore and café steady, and the pastries were getting low, despite Nina having ordered more. She made a note to arrange even more for next week. She had no idea if all Saturdays would be like this, but she wouldn't argue if they were. Saturday alone could keep her in business if it remained this busy.

Just after noon, Mandy wandered in again, smiling and greeting Nina by name as she ordered her coffee. She took her drink to a corner table, which she caught just as a woman with her two kids was leaving, and settled in with her books as usual. Nina didn't have much time to think about Mandy, but she did note the sparks of magic remained. And for some reason that made Nina feel better.

She was so busy, that when the handsome man with the great smile walked up to the counter, she blinked in surprise. She hadn't seen him come into the café at all, and the fact that she'd missed him was a testament to how busy they'd been.

"Hi," she said, feeling silly and ridiculous and smiling entirely too much.

"Hello there. Thought I'd give the place a try on the weekend. Actually take some time to wander the bookstore."

"Glad. Yeah. That's good. Hope it's been pleasant."

"It's been great." He chuckled as she slid his coffee mug across the counter to her. "Nice not to have to get a to-go cup this time." He gave her a nod and headed to a table near the front window.

Today he wasn't wearing a suit but instead had on casual jeans and a t-shirt. Nothing fancy, like his work clothes. But he still looked very nice. And that smile made Nina sigh.

Akira gave her a look, then winked before moving on to the next customer. Nina felt her cheeks heating. That she was so obvious—and at her age!—was just embarrassing.

The bell over the door dinged, a welcome distraction, and a man walked in who Nina vaguely recognized but it took her several moments to place him. She was pretty sure he hadn't been in the café before. But there was something about him that still nagged at the back of her mind.

Then it hit her that she'd seen him outside on the sidewalk a week ago, frowning at the store sign. He hadn't come in. She wasn't sure why she'd noticed him at all. But that was definitely where she remembered him from.

He glared around the coffee shop, his brows lowered as he scanned the tables. She watched him warily. Something about him set off her alarms.

Boo, who'd been sleeping on his stool next to the register, woke up and stretched on the way off the stool, landing lightly on the floor. He started toward the man, paused, the hair along his back rising, and while Boo rarely hissed at people, he did issue a low, nearly silent growl that had Nina immediately on alert.

"Stay here," she said to Akira, who looked confused by the order but still remained behind the counter as Nina rounded it.

"Can I help you?" she asked the man, stepping in front of him to draw his attention.

"What? No. Of course not. I'm looking for someone."

"Someone whose expecting you?" Nina stayed in front of him, blocking him from moving farther into the café. Boo wound around her ankles, his hackles still up.

"None of your business." The man snarled at her. "Who are you anyway?"

"The owner."

"Well, owner, this is none of your business."

"Sir, I'm just trying to help. But your attitude is a disruption to my café. I'm going to have to ask you to leave."

"You could try. But until I find her, I'm not going anywhere."

Nina hated that this was happening, and she hated the man in front of her challenging her this way. "Shall I call the police, sir?" Not that she thought the police would help at this stage. The man hadn't done anything but be rude so far.

Then she felt the magic around him starting to build.

"She stole something from me," the man said. "I'm just here to get it back."

"That's something you should take up with the proper

authorities," Nina said, even as she pulled a charm out from her t-shirt and let it hang over the front of her white apron. She rarely needed the shield these days, not since she'd gotten old enough to learn how to avoid conflicts. But this was her place, and no one was going to disrespect it. "Now I need you to leave."

Boo continued to weave around her ankles, the movements raising a charge of magic that raced along Nina's nerves and up to the charm, starting the small, silver pendant to glowing with bluish energy. No one but another magic wielder would see the glow. Everyone else in the café would simply see the owner confronting a difficult customer.

But the man was a magic wielder and he saw the glow.

He narrowed his eyes at her. "You're messing with the wrong man," he said, his voice low.

"I'm not 'messing' with anyone," she said. "You're no longer welcome in this café. I will ask one more time, and one more time only. Leave. Now."

The magic building along her skin tingled. She felt movement behind her. People in the crowded café scraping chairs and pushing against tables. Some of them standing, but not going anywhere. Others left toward the bookstore. She was aware of someone stepping up behind her, but her focus was on the man she knew for certain was a threat. She didn't need details. His aggressive grab for magic to intimidate her was all she needed.

Not in her café.

From behind her, she heard a quiet, "He's here for me. I

don't want this to cause trouble for your lovely coffee shop. Please. I'll deal with him."

Nina didn't have to turn to recognize Mandy's voice. "That's your choice of course," she said, "but you don't have to feel coerced into leaving. This man will be, however."

"She stole money from me. She stole…things."

"Things?"

"He thinks I took a book from him," Mandy said, her voice even lower. "I didn't."

"She's a liar!" He looked around Nina. "Give me back my book or—"

"Or what?" Nina asked. She let the magic rising over her skin build, Boo circling her ankles faster now. The magic fairly crackled around her.

The man took a step back, glaring. "You think you're strong enough to keep me out?" he hissed. "Child, I have more power than you can possibly imagine."

"If that were the case, you wouldn't be standing here throwing around threats," Nina said, equally quietly. "You'd have acted already. Which means you're in over your head. I suggest you leave. Leave this woman alone. And never show up here again. Or I will be forced to do…more."

The man snarled, lunged toward her, and got tossed backward against the front door. Hard enough the glass shivered and the bell overhead rang. More people behind her moved away, into the bookstore. She heard Akira on the phone, presumably calling for help.

"Like I said," Nina murmured. "You need to leave." She could feel the fine hairs along her neck and forehead starting to flutter as the power she and Boo built created its own kind of air currents.

"I'll have what's mine back!"

"Not going to let you threaten one of my regulars," Nina said.

She felt Mandy reach for her, but Nina raised a hand to stop her.

"She's a thief!" the man snarled. "She stole my—" He cut himself off, glancing around. Then he hissed so quietly, only Nina and Mandy would have heard him, "She stole my spell book and I will have it back."

"I did no such thing," Mandy said. "I don't even know what that is."

And yet Mandy had protective magic sparking off her. That raised its own questions. But those could wait.

"Again, that is something you can take up with the authorities," Nina said. "File a police report. Let them question her. But there will be no coercion or threats in my café. Do you understand?" She stepped closer and lowered her voice. "You've no idea what you're dealing with either, child," she mimicked his tone. "I suggest you take heed and find a different solution."

Suddenly, and without warning, the man lunged at Nina. She braced to hit him with a spell, but before she could gather the words, a large hand dropped onto the man's shoulder. "That's about enough of that," a deep voice said.

The power rising up around the man threatening Mandy should have made it impossible for a human to touch him. And yet. The man with the nice smile very firmly took hold of the threatening man's shoulders and shoved him toward the door.

Nina made a little move with her hand, and the door swung open, giving the lawyer room to shove the other man out into the street.

Nina made another gesture with her fingers, and the door closed. Locking shut to the threatening man when he tried to get back inside.

He glared, pounded the glass. And then a car drove up behind him on the road. A big, black SUV with darkly tinted windows.

Swinging around, the man started shouting a denial. A large burly man and an equally large and burly woman stepped out of the black SUV, grabbed the threatening man by the arms, and shoved him back into the SUV before Nina could do more than blink. The burly man climbed in behind the threatening man. The burly woman gave Nina a little head nod, then got into the passenger's side of the car. The SUV drove away a beat later, moving into traffic at a carefully lawful pace.

Leaving Nina, Mandy, and the lawyer with the nice smile staring after it.

* * *

"Well that was weird," Nina murmured in the silence following the threatening man's disappearance—possible abduction.

"Very," the man with the nice smile agreed.

They both turned to look at Mandy. Boo gave them all a look, then returned to his stool, hopping up and circling around to find a comfortable position, then settling in to nap.

Nina mostly ignored him. They could talk about what happened later. First, she really wanted to know what Mandy knew.

Mandy's cheeks heated and she shrugged. "He's one of my professors. I'm studying ancient civilizations through the lens of their religious rituals. Professor Wagner has a lot of interesting books in his office so I've scanned them while waiting on him for meetings. But I *never* took anything from his office. I don't even know what he's talking about. He's been accusing me of stealing this book for a month now. I kept expecting him to take it up with the university, but…" She shrugged. "He never went to any officials or the police or anything. I kept telling him I didn't have his book. He started getting…aggressive."

"And that's when you got the protective charm?" Nina asked, then winced. Oops. The lawyer probably didn't know magic existed and had been a part of all this.

Mandy looked a little confused, too. "Protective charm? You mean my necklace?" She pulled a necklace out from the collar of her t-shirt. A small silver medallion hung from a silver chain, not unlike Nina's own charm. Though Mandy's was a simple circle with a five-pointed star in the center. The silver ran with blue magic, and it sparked like static around Mandy when she held it up. She didn't appear to feel any of the magic, though.

"A nice older lady handed this to me…last week, I think?

She said she'd seen the professor arguing with me on the street before I came into the bookstore. She said it was a good luck charm, which made me laugh and I told her what I was studying. She insisted I take the charm so…I did." Mandy frowned as she looked at the silver medallion. "I guess I must have accepted it, but to be honest, I don't remember that part. Just that I was wearing it the next time I came out of my apartment, and I felt safer. And the professor wasn't following me around anymore."

Still frowning, she looked at Nina as if Nina might have some answers to the hanging questions. Nina did not. Though she had some suspicions. "I don't suppose this older woman was in here last night? The one you sat with near closing time. She drank tea. Had interesting reading material."

"That's her! Yes. Do you know her?"

"Not personally." But Nina intended on getting to know her because she sounded like Nina's kind of person. "But it sounds like the charm was good luck for you."

"I suppose." Mandy winced. "I'm sorry about the scene, though."

Nina waved that away. "It wasn't your fault. And he won't be allowed back here again, so you'll be safe to return if you want to." Nina would spell the door to ensure that particular professor never got into her café again.

Although, given the big black SUV, and the nod from the burly woman, Nina had a feeling Professor Wagner wasn't going to be making another appearance any time soon.

"Thank you," Mandy said. "For your help and everything." She smiled at the lawyer. "And thank you."

"You're very welcome. Glad I could assist." He handed Mandy a card. "And if he does attempt to press charges for theft, and you need a lawyer, call me. If I can't help, I'll be happy to refer you to someone."

"Oh, I wouldn't be able to afford—"

"No cost," the lawyer said. "Pro bono for a fellow coffee addict."

Mandy grinned and tucked the card away. "Thank you again. Both of you. I knew I would love this place. I'm glad I started coming here."

"Tell you what," Nina said. "To make up for all the drama, free coffees on the house for everyone."

A general cheer went up, which made Nina chuckle. She glanced at Boo long enough to see his smirk before he closed his eyes and went back to napping, or appearing to nap.

Mandy joined the other handful of people still inside the café at the counter as Akira worked quickly to make a lot of coffee. Nina needed to go help, but first…

"Thank you," she said to the lawyer. Then narrowed her eyes and lowered her voice. "How did you manage to touch him?"

Whatever magic the professor had been dealing in, an ordinary human shouldn't have been able to touch him and toss him out so easily. The burly people had grabbed Professor Wagner, but they weren't here for Nina to ask. The lawyer was.

The lawyer shrugged, and winced, and looked away. "I… might be more than a lawyer." He gave her a look, a kind of narrow-eyed, hesitant, expectant look she could relate to.

It was the look of a person trying to admit something without admitting it just in case the person they were talking to didn't believe in things like magic.

Nina nodded, leaned closer and lowered her voice to admit, "I might be more than a café owner."

"I had a feeling." He glanced at Boo. "Nice cat. Seems very…familiar."

"Good way to put it." Nina raised her brows hopefully. "So does this mean we haven't scared you off?"

"Not a chance."

Oh good. "So… Can I ask you something else?"

"Sure."

"What is your name?"

He grinned. And Nina sighed.

He really did have a nice smile.

HENRY AT THE CAFÉ

HENRY

Watching the busy movement between café and bookstore, Henry let out a breath and tried not to tap his foot. There was plenty of time still. He checked the pocket watch attached to his vest. Yes. Plenty of time still. No reason to be impatient.

The lovely owner of the café brought him his coffee, black with a lot of sugar, and set it down on the table beside his elbow. "Everything okay?" she asked. "How were the croissants?"

"Perfection as always," he said.

Her gaze narrowed and Henry realized he'd made a mistake.

Fortunately, as a witch, Nina was used to people with secrets and was always careful not to ask whenever he made a mistake. He very much admired that about her.

She smiled and nodded as if he hadn't just said something wrong, and returned to the counter, giving her giant Maine coon familiar a little scratch on the head to maintain the illusion that he was an ordinary cat.

Was he supposed to know that in this time? He couldn't remember.

He made a little mental note to himself to leave Nina a better tip than he had last time. Last time he'd been so distracted. He was a little distracted this time as well. Par for the course, really. Always distracted. Always something on his mind. Sometimes that something wasn't the right here-and-now either. But that came with the job.

He pulled the watch out of his vest pocket again, though he knew he still had several minutes. The watch was a lovely old heirloom. At the moment, it was mostly silver with some darker black shading to highlight the swirling Celtic knot design. Those weren't always there. Sometimes the design was a simple rose. Sometimes an exploding star. Sometimes abstract lines. It really depended. Sometimes the watch wasn't silver. Sometimes it rested on his wrist.

He liked when it was a pocket watch, though. The aesthetic pleased him. And it went very well with his embroidered navy vest.

The seconds hand ticked away, bringing the minute hand one more tiny black notch closer to the time.

Henry looked toward the bookstore again. One more minute.

When that moment happened, he didn't have to look at the watch. He could feel The Time in his bones.

He rose and took the three steps forward that were necessary.

Tanya Alvarez slammed into him, just as she was supposed to.

"Oh, I'm so sorry!" She held his elbow as he regained his balance.

He feigned a wobble and then smiled. "Not at all. Entirely my fault. Wasn't watching where I was going." He gave her hand a pat. She was a lovely young woman. Dark hair still, though it would be gray the last time he saw her. Or was that next time? He couldn't remember.

In this moment, she was young. Two years left in her residency. Flustered and tired and desperately in need of a break. Which was why she was here after her long, overnight shift in the ER instead of home and asleep.

Henry patted his vest and then gave a sharp nod. "All as it should be. And you, my dear. Are you okay?"

"Fine. Thank you." Her eyes welled for a moment before she took a deep breath and sucked the tears back in.

There would come a time when she forgets to cry. And a time when she remembers again. Henry thought the crying was better for her. But that wasn't his place to say.

She carried a small, reusable canvas bag with the bookstore logo on it, with two paperbacks inside. Henry gestured to the bag, the seconds ticking loudly in his head. "I hope you found something entertaining to read."

She glanced at the bag and smiled. "A couple of Romance novels."

"Ah, the guaranteed happy ending. I love those."

She grinned. "So do I. May I be honest?"

"Of course."

"You stuck me as more a reader of literature with a capital L."

Henry laughed. A genuine laugh. Dr. Alvarez was a delight. "I like all books," he said. "But I especially love happy endings."

She nodded. "Me too."

The last second ticked past and Henry let out a quiet, relieved breath. "Well. I don't mean to keep you. My apologies again for bumping into you."

"No, no. It was me."

He waved away her protest. "I hope you enjoy your happy ending," he said, returning to his seat.

If Dr. Tanya Alvarez noticed that he'd been heading one way and never went that way after their collision, she didn't comment. She hurried to the counter and ordered a coffee. She'd barely received her to-go cup, when a loud screeching noise from outside echoed through the café followed by the sound of metal crunching metal.

Everyone ran to the café window. Henry walked. Outside, a car had driven up onto the sidewalk and slammed into the, fortunately, empty covered bus stop. The driver climbed out of the car, rubbing his neck. Dr. Alvarez hurried outside to help.

Henry stood at the window, watching as several pedestrians and Dr. Alvarez tended to the shaken driver.

When Nina moved up beside him, he said, "His breaks failed. No one's fault. Just a horrible accident."

"Could have been worse," Nina said, her gaze fixed on the ongoing events outside. "That woman who was just collecting her coffee when the accident happened… She said that was her bus stop."

"Was it? Well, it's fortunate she wasn't there already, wasn't it."

"Fortunate." Nina glanced at him from the corner of her eye. Henry glanced back in the same manner.

He gave in first. "In three days time, she'll stop one of the surgeons in the ER from making a mistake that would cost a young woman her life."

"Ah," Nina said as if she understood completely.

And he'd dare say, she did. "That young woman will go on to do great things later in her life. Things that would not happen without her."

"Important things?"

"Important things." He gave Nina a look. "And she's just the first person Dr. Alvarez saves in her extraordinary career."

"Then I'm very glad Dr. Alvarez was conveniently delayed and not in the bus stop when the car hit it."

"Yes. That would have been very unfortunate." Henry smiled, then checked his pocket watch. The Celtic knot pattern was now one of the sunburst patterns. And there were some gold accents in the design. He liked this one, too. "Well. It seems it's time for me to get going. Thank you, again, for the coffee and wonderful pastries."

"You're welcome," Nina said. "Another time?"

Henry tipped his head. "Another time."

Though which time, he wasn't entirely sure.

Yet.

AGNES AT THE CAFÉ

AGNES

gnes Waters had been on this planet for a very long time. Longer than most people would think possible. Even the lovely witch proprietor of the café, Nina. Maybe even her familiar, the Maine coon, Boo, would have a hard time believing how long Agnes had been alive. Nina herself was quite a bit older than she let on, of course. Maybe in a hundred years, she'd be able to understand Agnes's existence.

Most didn't, though. And that was for the best.

Agnes had also had many names over the years. Monikers that fit her surroundings, her era, her presentation. She was quite fond of her current name. It felt a bit antique to her, and she liked things that other people considered antique as she'd been around when those things were not.

She also loved Nina's little café attached to an adorable independent bookstore and had been coming here regularly since it opened. This was her happy spot. The tea was good. The bookstore stocked plenty of erotica and erotic poetry books—though Agnes suspected the proprietor of the bookstore got in fresh publications especially for Agnes at this stage. And when Agnes tired of erotica, there was a substantial section of yummy Romances to choose from. A delightful genre. She'd been happy to see it's evolution over the centuries. This modern incarnation was quite entertaining.

Nina got in a selection of very nice teas as well. Getting nice tea could sometimes be complicated. And Agnes had been addicted to the stuff since her first cup in China, where she'd been when it began to emerge as a drink and not just an addition to soups or part of medicinal concoctions. She didn't talk about that time of course. There were very few beings alive who would remember that period. Maybe some of the older dragons? But most of them were asleep. Few others would be able to trace back that far.

Occasionally, Agnes felt her age, and the fact that she couldn't talk about certain things with anyone who might understand, who had actually been there. That was the side effect of aging anyway, though. Even humans experienced that. So she didn't dwell on it. Life was a buffet of choices and interesting things to experience. No point in crying over things that could not be changed. Time marched in one direction for most of them, and she was bound by that forward momentum as much as everyone else.

On that particular afternoon in the café, though, her peaceful reading and excellent tea were disrupted by one of the few humans on the planet who understood Agnes and her age. Aidan still didn't know what Agnes Waters was because Agnes wasn't inclined to discuss that with her. But Aidan was no ordinary human and her understanding of things, even when she didn't *know* the thing, was rather impressive.

Aidan was not impressive to look upon, however. She was as ordinary as a woman could be in these times. Her brown hair was neither long nor short, not too dark, not too light. She was a middling height, maybe a little above average but not so much as to be noticeable. She was neither skinny nor fat. She was not attractive enough to turn heads but wasn't notably ugly either. She had no tattoos, no piercings, no moles, no birthmarks to latch onto as a distinguishing feature.

She dressed casually in jeans and a t-shirt this fine spring morning and blended in so well with the other women scattered around the café as to be entirely easy to overlook.

Aidan was so absolutely perfect at blending into her surroundings that no one took any notice of her. And if Aidan wished to take that even farther, she could literally will people not to see her. Which, even Agnes had to admit, was a lovely trick. One she'd practiced herself a few centuries ago and gotten quite adept at before abandoning the effort. She, personally, couldn't be bothered.

Aidan's ability to be so absolutely ordinary and unremarkable, though, was truly awe-inspiring. And if one didn't look too closely at her eyes, didn't notice that hint of red in the depth of the brown—or wrote it off as a trick of the light—one might not ever even remember Aidan after encountering her.

Agnes, for her part, had never forgotten her first encounter with the demon hunter.

"Well, well, well." She smiled and nodded at the chair across from her. "What brings you to my current favorite hangout?"

Aidan sank into the comfortable wooden seat and smiled. "You say 'hangout' feels like an anacronyms."

"One must use modern language. It's important."

"Of course. One must try at least."

Agnes snorted, rolling her eyes at the hunter. "Well with that said, what does bring you to my corner of the world? I don't imagine this visit is purely coincidental."

"It's not. Mores the pity." Aidan glanced around. "This seems like a very comfortable…hangout. Nice place. Bookstores well stocked and friendly, too."

"You can see why I enjoy my time here, then."

"I do."

"And why I might not want anything to happen here that would make it difficult for me to come back."

"Not here to upset the apple cart as they say. Things go to plan, you should be able to return tomorrow with none the wiser."

"In that case, I believe an explanation is in order. Would you like a coffee? Tea?"

"Don't suppose they have sodas? I could do with a Coke."

"Ah. You're on a hunt?"

Aidan gave her a slight nod.

"Someone here?"

"Not yet. Arriving soon, though."

"A meeting you arranged."

"No. But this…person is an old acquaintance of yours."

"Ah." Well. Wasn't that inconvenient. "He's violated his terms of sanctuary."

"He has."

"That hardly seems credible."

Aidan shrugged. "Nevertheless. Here I am."

"Yes."

Aidan wouldn't be here if Agnes's former *acquaintance* hadn't done something to earn the demon hunter's attention. There were rules for a demon claiming this planet as sanctuary. Rules that had to be abided—and really, they weren't *that* difficult—or the sanctuary contract was violated and the hunters began hunting the demon again.

A complicated and tiresome process, really. She'd seen it in action. Hunters might die. The demon might be banished. Really, it was easier for the demon to just abide by the rules of sanctuary. There were so many freedoms afforded. More than Agnes thought truly deserved. They were demons after all.

"Are you here to recruit me into the hunt?" Agnes said. She tried to stay out of demon and demon hunter affairs because they were always messy. But eventually, Agnes got drawn in to most things. Impossible to avoid all the things when your lifetime spanned millennia.

"Not necessarily," Aidan said as Agnes signaled for Nina. "I'm here because my quarry will be here soon. Finding you present is…an interesting twist. Especially given this particular quarry."

"Mm. Interesting." A complicated word, that one. In whatever language it was used.

Nina joined them and Agnes asked if she had any sodas.

"Not diet," Adian added. "Regular Coke would be great."

"I actually happen to have some regular Coke on hand," Nina said, and her eyes narrowed at Aidan. "I had a shipment delivered on accident yesterday. Decided to keep them just in case. Never know when someone might want one, right?"

"I'd be very grateful, thank you," Aidan said, her smile neutral and the slight red in the depth of her eyes dancing.

Nina glanced at Agnes. Agnes could see the half-question, half-understanding there. She probably did know what demon hunters were. Might even know the legendary hunter sitting across from Agnes. At least she'd know her by name if names had been exchanged. But like all the best proprietors, Nina kept her speculation and questions to herself and got Aidan's drink without any further comment.

She didn't ask if Aidan wanted anything to eat, though, and it was her usual habit to offer a pastry with the drinks she served. Which confirmed for Agnes that Nina knew what was about to happen.

Most hunters didn't eat right before a fight with a demon. There could be…smells involved and visuals that would cause the unwary hunter to, as they say, toss up their cookies. The less there was to toss up, the better.

"While we wait, perhaps you'd tell me a little story," Agnes said, cupping her tea mug in both hands, her book abandoned for the moment to one side of the little round wooden table. Bookmarked because she couldn't abide bent pages.

"What kind of story would you like?" Aidan asked, her gaze dancing to the door once before she settled her attention fully on Agnes.

"A tale of two demons, perhaps." Agnes smiles. "A violation of sanctuary."

Agnes didn't bother limiting what she said for fear those around her would overhear. Aidan would will the café patrons not to hear. It was probably better Aidan didn't expend much will just then, even for the sake of their privacy. But as Agnes had begun to think of this place as her place, and there was going to be a demon fight here soon, she wanted answers.

Especially since this involved someone Agnes had once spent time with.

"He killed a hunter," Aidan said. "One who…was new enough that this particular demon should have known better. The hunter wasn't coming for him. The hunter was issuing a warning. And instead of just taking the warning. He killed the hunter."

There had to be more to the story because this particular demon had been on Earth, availing of sanctuary, for several centuries now. The rule about not killing or interfering with demon hunters should honestly have been the easiest of all rules to follow. Why bother when you essentially have the run of the place?

So to kill a hunter, an egregious act that would absolutely

lead to banishment from this realm, Agnes thought her former acquaintance might have been pushed into a corner.

Not that that made things better or earned her sympathy. Her acquaintance was an asshole, and she wouldn't mourn him being banished back to a demon realm. Still…

She didn't like that Aidan was being evasive.

Maybe she wasn't. Maybe this was all she knew about the situation.

Agnes doubted that, though.

"And his twin?" Agnes asked. "What of his sanctuary?"

"He isn't the one involved in the killing. His sanctuary hasn't been violated."

And wasn't that also, as they say, interesting. Because the brother was the very reason the twins had asked for sanctuary. The brother was…not a demon made for demon realms. Artistic, weak—for a demon—and not at all bloodthirsty. Unlike his asshole brother. Who was happy to kill and torture and torment like any ordinary demon. The twin, on the other hand, fit in perfectly in a human world. Less intent on torture, more intent on…climbing ladders, as they might say. But artistic ladders. Not power ladders. Other demons moved along those assents and were happy to run their little corners of the human realm. The twin, though… His ambitions lay in the realm of the arts.

It had always struck Agnes as mildly ironic. A few centuries ago, this twin was well known for producing religious art.

Demons weren't what certain current religions claimed them to be. Not fallen angels rebelling against a god. Not mysterious elements of nature out to get humans. They were beings from different realms, horrible realms with horrible beings populating them. Very few redeeming qualities to those places that Agnes could ever see. Lots of death and torture. And the human realm was such a ripe place full of creatures that feared death and torture—fear that fed the demons as surely as the physical bodies—that demons loved being summoned here. At least most of them did.

At any rate, they were, like most other beings, driven by their hungers and their hungers were destructive and violent and evil. But they weren't part of a particular human *religion*.

They did like to use religious beliefs to their benefit, though. The twin had used those beliefs in his art. And had won many accolades and wealth because of it. Not that the wealth mattered. He was always and only after the accolades.

His brother, the one more…demon presenting, as the kids might say, liked the wealth. They'd actually made a very fine team here. Because the artistic twin could survive this place. He was not long for survival in any of the demon realms. Even with the muscle and violence of his brother to protect him.

That was why they'd sought sanctuary here. Here, the artistic twin was not "weak" compared to humans. Here he wasn't the prey.

That the asshole brother would risk sanctuary, and his twin's life, by violating the rules truly was a mystery.

One Agnes intended on solving before the hunt was concluded.

"Interesting," Agnes said.

"Yes," Aidan said. "I thought so, too."

And so, the hunter wasn't saying as much as she knew.

Agnes wondered if Aidan would have said more, had they been given more time. But just then, her former acquaintance, the asshole twin demon, stepped into the café.

D emons with enough power, and with the intention of remaining in the human realm, did not show themselves as demons when walking around. That would surely bring the human world down upon them. Hardly the point.

No. Demons who claimed sanctuary and walked among humans freed from the bonds of a summoning contract presented themselves as human. The type of human façade they choose depended on the demon, their vanity, their desire for camouflage or display.

In this, both twins were of a single mind. They chose display.

Remarkably handsome, young and healthy façades that blended into current ideas of attractiveness. Last time Agnes had seen her acquaintance, he'd been favoring the dandy display, full of big white wigs and embroidered, velvet clothing, and high heels and glittery jewelry. There were lace handkerchiefs and heavy gold rings with imbedded precious stones to add even more glamour to the outfits. His jaw had been narrow and his features sharp and full of cutting beauty. The image of the elegant, nobleman.

He had changed that look for this century. His features were still sharp, and beautiful, but he'd adopted short, black hair and blue eyes and pale skin to go with his finely tailored black suit and tie. Everything sleek and minimal. Even the thick silver pinky ring he wore was elegantly understated. A display of casual, modern wealth. Not old school money.

And he did not look a day over forty.

Agnes rolled her eyes. None of them appreciated the benefits of an older, mature appearance. The way one could…blend in when perceived as "older."

But she knew that would defeat the purpose for both twins. Their point was to stand out. And they did.

This one, the asshole, the money-making, power-climbing, violent one, went by Charles Richard Holmes the Third the last time she'd met him. She had no idea what name he'd adopted in this century.

Like Agnes, he went through multiple names and multiple identities. Those who lived long, and didn't want to be noticed for it, were forced into identity changes very few decades.

He spotted her first, his smile almost a smirk. They'd parted on reasonable terms but with the intention to never see each other again. This wouldn't be a pleasant reunion. But they hadn't parted enemies. Agnes had simply decided she wanted nothing more to do with either Charles—whoever he was in this century—or his brother. Who'd gone by Patrick O'Brien last they'd met. Though the two demons looked quite alike in their demon form, they never presented themselves to the human world as twins and therefore always looked quite different, even when taking on guises from similar backgrounds for the purpose of their latest scheme.

Charles's gaze jumped to Aidan and his smirk fell. But to Agnes's surprise, he didn't snarl and scowl or even grin. His expression went neutral.

He didn't hesitate to approach their table, taking a seat to one side, placing himself between Aidan and Agnes.

From the corner of her eye, Agnes was aware of Nina quietly ushering people out of the café with some quite interesting excuses—flash book sale, don't want to miss that; small water leak in the back, no coffee for a bit; heard there's a film being shot down the street, probably want to go see what's happening.

Agnes had a feeling Nina was tailoring her excuses to suit the individual patron, and wasn't that a very neat trick. She wondered what excuse Nina would have tried on her, had she not been involved in the imminent demon fight.

Charles gave Agnes a nod and raised his brows at her.

"Agnes Waters," she introduced. She couldn't even remember what name he might have known her by the last time they'd spoken. Something befitting the era, she was sure.

"Charles Lewis," he introduced.

"Charles?" Still? How unusual. But then, he'd always been the less creative brother. At least when it came to this sort of thing. His creativity for torture on the other hand…

"It's a family name," he said by way of excuse.

"Of course. I understand you've done something to

complicate your family situation, though." Agnes let her gaze move to Aidan.

Aidan hadn't bothered to speak yet. She just stared at Charles, her expression bland and unreadable.

"I wanted Agnes...Ms. Waters here as a neutral third party to our negotiation," Charles said to Aidan. "That's why we're meeting here."

"I had wondered about that," Aidan said.

As had Agnes.

"Why do you need a neutral third party?" Aidan asked. "And what do you think we're here to negotiate?"

"My violation of sanctuary rules is not what it seems."

"Everyone says that."

"No," Charles said with a little head shake. "Everyone does not. If they violate the rules, they've done it thinking they can simply kill all the hunters that come for them."

Aidan nodded her head from side to side, a half acknowledgement of that truth. "Some of them. Yes. Some of them... The weaker ones always have an excuse. A reason why they shouldn't be sent back."

"I'm not one of the weaker ones."

"Your twin is," Aidan said. She raised a hand when Charles opened his mouth to speak. "But his sanctuary isn't void. He's allowed to stay."

Charles let out a sigh that. If Agnes were the generous sort, she'd all relieved. He hadn't been certain his brother would be able to remain. That was interesting.

"I am...grateful for that."

"As I understand it," Aidan said, "you purposefully asked

for individual contracts for you and your brother. Purposefully ensured your sanctuary and his would not be bound up together. Had you always intended on violating yours?"

"No." Almost a scowl, quickly controlled. Aidan had hit a soft spot.

Agnes found that interesting, too. In fact, all of this was quite interesting. Even better than the book she'd been reading.

"But there was always the possibility that this realm wouldn't suit… And we'd have to go different ways." Charles's expression tightened, his mouth flattening into a line. "Unfortunately, I didn't realize that wouldn't be possible until too late."

"Meaning?" This from Agnes. She leaned forward on the table, cupping her hands under her chin. She was riveted.

"They're twins and they can't be separated in different realms," Aidan supplied.

"You knew all along?" Charles asked.

"No. You just said as much."

"What does this mean to his violation of sanctuary, then?" Agnes asked. That the twins couldn't be separated in different realms was not something Charles had ever admitted to her. She wondered if he'd even known back then. Perhaps not.

"You're hoping the fact that you can't be separated, but your brother's contract hasn't been violated, that you'll be able to stay?" Aidan asked.

"Not…" Charles's nose twitched.

A tic Agnes couldn't quite interpret. He didn't smell of brimstone or sulfur, as one might assume a demon did, but of very expensive cologne. However, in that moment, some of the façade slipped. A little flare of red in the eyes. A little hint of something burning crept in around the edges of the expensive cologne and tailored appearance.

"The hunter I killed," Charles said, more quietly, "threatened my brother and I."

"How?" Aidan didn't immediately deny the charge.

"He said freed demons were an abomination, and he was there to banish us."

"He couldn't have, not unless he had the voided contract."

"I was aware."

"Then no need to kill him."

"He… The hunter attacked my brother."

Aidan shrugged. "Your brother is strong enough to fend off a human attack."

"Not a hunter attack."

That might well be true. Agnes wasn't sure. She'd seen the hunters do impressive things. Especially Aidan. A hunter's will was their superpower. The thing they used against a demon. The fights were often just a clash of wills and the strongest will won. That a hunter could survive those fights, win those tests of will, with a demon was a testament to their strength. Will beyond what most humans could conjure. Their ability to wield their wills often resembled magic. And to be a living hunter, one had to have a will that could best a demon.

It was entirely possible this hunter had such inner power.

"Your defense is…self-defense?" Aidan asked.

"No. My defense is protecting my brother from a hunter gone rogue."

Aidan leaned back in her chair. Her half empty glass of Coke now ignored. Agnes couldn't remember Aidan even drinking any of it.

When the hunter didn't immediately react to the charge of a hunter gone rogue, Agnes started to grow suspicious. What did Aidan know that she wasn't admitting to? She hadn't outright denied the claim or even told Charles to fuck off with his excuses. Which is something Agnes might have done, and certainly would have expected from a demon hunter.

That Aidan was considering him, her expression contemplative and not hostile, even though he was a literal demon, had Agnes considering the situation closer too.

She knew the rules for sanctuary. She knew of the contracts and the bargains made for a demon to remain free in this world. She knew the hunters had rules around all this too—and everyone knew that was for the hunters' safety.

Why would a hunter break those rules, and then choose to go after one of the least objectionable freed demons? There were plenty doing much worse things than creating art and then selling it for exorbitant prices. Plenty doing the things Charles would probably do more of if not for his brother.

Why go after Charles' twin?

"Was it revenge for something you did?" Agnes asked. "Your brother confused for you?" Even though the twins never presented as looking alike here in their human forms, a hunter would know the relationship. She supposed there was an outside chance for confusion between the two.

But Charles shook his head. "The hunter claimed all freed demons were an abomination and wanted them all banished."

"But why your brother specifically?" Aidan asked, taking up Agnes's line of questioning. "He's not as strong as you, but he's also not doing anything particularly harmful except taking full advantage of a capitalist system to sell his art. Can't blame him for that. There are human CEOs who commit actual crimes in the name of capitalism. You've done worse things than your brother."

"I can only assume he went for him because he assumed he'd be easy. Assumed he could banish him, despite not having a broken contract."

"There are weaker freed demons claiming sanctuary," Aidan said.

"Some very weak as to be almost human," Agnes added.

There were some freed demons walking this earth who just wanted to avoid the demons that would kill them. They were the reason sanctuary had been created—or at least they were the ones who served the purpose of sanctuary. They lived quiet, human-like lives, got jobs, paid taxes, some even got married. There were no children from most of those marriages. Demons rarely reproduced with humans, and when they did, the result for the human was rarely good. But those quiet, weak demons otherwise harmed no one and just lived their lives.

Over the last few centuries, Agnes had even met two of

those freed demons. Lovely people, really. Keeping their heads down and keeping their evil impulses to themselves.

If Agnes were being mercenary, she'd have said those demons were the perfect ones for a rogue demon hunter to go after. One less freed demon, even if the demon had done nothing to be banished back to a certain death in the demon realms.

"I need to know why this rogue went after your brother if I'm to judge this case properly," Agnes said aloud. "It is the part of your tale that is most illogical and leads me to believe you or your brother actually did violate sanctuary."

Charles let out a huff, and with it came the faintest scent of brimstone. A tell that he was growing frustrated and was upset.

"I can't tell you what I don't know," he snapped.

"Then I can't rule in your favor or take your word the hunter actually had gone rogue," Agnes said. "We may be old acquaintances, but a hunter's word must be taken over a demon's when considering how excellent demons are at lying."

"Hunters lie too."

"Of course. Everyone lies." Even her. Maybe especially her. Her name wasn't even really Agnes Waters. "My point is still valid. Given the natures of the two parties involved, the more reliable narrative will come from a hunter. Even though that hunter is dead, he was still a hunter who specifically went after your brother for a violation of sanctuary. This is more believable than that he just went rogue."

Now Charles ran a hand up through his hair, a gesture

that ruffled the previous smooth style. It was probably the most discombobulated Agnes had ever seen the demon.

"He…was not a good hunter," Charles said.

"You're not helping your case. Of course a demon would think that."

"Objectively. He was a bad man."

"Again—"

"Yes," Charles interrupted with a hiss. "Alright, alright. Just…" He looked between Agnes and Aidan, who'd remained silently watching the exchange.

That Aidan still hadn't contributed a comment on whether the hunter was good or not was fascinating to Agnes. She'd known Aidan hadn't been completely open about what she knew of the situation. But Anges's curiosity about what the hunter *did* know was rising with every passing moment. Oh, she'd love to get a look into that woman's head.

But that violated Agnes's rules for herself, so…

Charles let out a long breath and said, "The hunter chose us because we're linked. Two demons with one stone, so to speak. Send one back, the other would have to go back. Get one of us to violate our sanctuary, both would be banished."

"And?" Agnes said, finally picking up her tea to sip. Here came the good stuff.

"And, he wasn't alone. He was sent." Here Charles glanced at Aidan. "You have a problem building inside the hunters."

Aidan stared back without comment.

Charles continued. "There's a faction who do not want any freed demons here, no matter how harmless we are."

Agnes snort-laughed into her tea, which brought Charles's scowl and Aidan's raised brows.

"Forgive me," she said. "But harmless and demon really aren't words that go together in the same sentence."

Charles had enough awareness to look chagrined and nod. "Nevertheless," he said. "Some of us have been scrupulous about abiding by our deals with the hunters." Aidan raised her brows again and Charles allowed, "Some of us push the limits of those deals to breaking point, but we still remain firmly inside the boundaries of our agreements. I would never have killed a hunter. Never. Because it would risk my brother's sanctuary here."

"Then why did you this time?" This from Aidan but asked quietly.

"The faction that wants us all banished… They sent in that young hunter knowing he'd fail. They sacrificed him to get me to break sanctuary. He…he was prepared to sacrifice a human, to blame my brother for that sacrifice. He stood there with a knife to a…to a young woman's neck, prepared to kill her and blame us."

"So you killed him to save the woman?" Aidan asked quietly. "Not to save your brother?"

"No. To save my brother. He'd have been sent back if the hunter had succeeded in framing him."

Agnes considered Charles closer. He was a demon. He was evil at his core. She was pretty sure he hadn't cared about the random human woman's life all that much. Agnes had spent time with him during an era when human life was…expendable, and he'd shown no particular interest in rectifying that state of affairs. And, if she were being honest with herself, human life was often quiet expendable, even to other humans, in most eras of human existence.

Still, Charles had never shown any signs of this bothering him. A single woman's life ended would be just one of thousands he'd witnessed. Hundreds of thousands over the centuries. Probably in the millions, now she considered it.

So she thought he was probably being as honest as a demon was capable of, saying that he hadn't killed the hunter to save the human's life but instead to save his brother's. Yet the outcome had been the same. He'd killed a hunter and saved an innocent human.

That very much complicated things if true.

"Any proof of this life you saved?" Agnes asked, really curious if he'd actually kept a human woman alive, or if he'd killed the hunter after the hunter had killed the woman.

Charles, looking as uncomfortable as Agnes had ever seen him, raised his hand.

A woman who'd been sitting at a table near the front window of the café stood and came over to them. The only person left in the café who Nina hadn't managed to usher out.

Tall, robust, red hair in a riot of curls around a dark tan complexion. Freckles across her cheeks. Probably in her mid-thirties. Dressed in jeans and a t-shirt with a glitter dragon on it. She had been sitting in that seat by the window since Agnes had arrived, sipping her drink and watching the pedestrians. Old habits for Agnes to take note of all the people in the café, but she hadn't spotted this woman as anyone she should pay attention to. And the woman hadn't appeared to be following the conversation. She hadn't looked up when Charles had entered the café. She'd shown no signs of acknowledgement.

"My name is Jessica," the woman said. "Jessica Vasquez. I understand Charles is in trouble for saving my life."

"Do you know who Charles is?" Aidan asked, her expression kind and neutral. No accusations but no instant sympathy either.

"I know who his brother is. I've worked for Winston, as a model, for the last three years."

"More than a model?" Agnes asked.

Jessica flicked a look to Agnes, but then turned her full focus of her attention back to Aidan. "We grew more personally involved over the last year." She glanced down before firming her lips and looking up at Aidan again. "I knew he was a…what he was before we got personally involved. I learned Charles was his brother and not just his manager not long after."

"What happened with the man who came to confront Charles and Winston?" Aidan asked.

"He said they were evil, accused me of being enthrall to Winston, and claimed he was going to set me free."

"How?"

"By killing me." She blinked hard a few times but held Aidan's gaze.

Agnes found this impressive and brave because she could practically feel Aidan's will now, pouring off of her as a physical thing… Willing the young woman to tell the truth.

Honestly, the hunter's will was so strong, Agnes felt the urge to reveal truths as well. Very impressive.

She watched Charles shift a little in his chair, obviously feeling the compulsion of Aidan's will as well. Agnes wondered what truths he was trying not to reveal in that moment. She smirked at him and sipped her tea when he scowled at her.

"I'm telling the truth," Jessica said.

"Yes." Aidan nodded. "The man who came to 'save you' from Winston intended on killing you."

"He did."

"And then what happened?"

"Charles killed the man."

"Did any other people come in after this happened?"

"No. No one else was there. Just the…man with the knife."

"Hm." Aidan held Jessica's gaze a moment longer. Then she looked to Agnes and raised her brows.

"Are you asking if I believe the child? Of course. How could I not after that…display?" She waved her hands vaguely at Aidan.

"Charles picked this place for our confrontation so you could be the impartial judge," Aidan said, smiling a little. "What say you, impartial judge?"

"I say he killed a man who was a serious threat to innocent life. Maybe not for any good or decent reason as we might know it." She gave Jessica a nod. "I don't mean to be cruel, but I don't think he did that for your sake."

"He didn't," Jessica said with a shrug. "It was for his brother."

"Well. It's nice to know you haven't been blinded by… love?"

Jessica's expression went through a series of emotions, all of which ended in a sort of confused mashup of conflicting feelings. "I wouldn't call what I have with Winston that."

"Really?" Agnes sipped her tea. This was turning into a delightful afternoon. "At any rate. It seems obvious to me Charles was acting in the right, and wouldn't have violated sanctuary if not pushed to protect a human life."

"I agree," Aidan said, meeting Charles's gaze.

His head turned to her so sharply Agnes could swear she heard his neck muscles twang. "You believe me?"

"I believe Jessica," Aidan said. "And Agnes has been around long enough to be a good judge of character."

"So…" Charles looked between Agnes and Aidan again. "What does this mean?"

"We don't need to test our wills against one another," Aidan said. "This time."

Agnes hid her amusement in her cup when Charles actually looked relieved at that comment. She'd known Charles for a very long time and knew exactly what kind of demon he was. She wouldn't have put money on him beating Aidan in a fight of wills either.

"What will you do about this faction of hunters?" Charles said. "How do I know they won't come after my brother again?"

"They won't," Aidan said. "You've my word."

Charles blinked hard at this, sitting back in his seat. So did Agnes.

Hunters only gave their word rarely because it meant something very serious to them. They never gave their word casually. Certainly not to demons. Not ever.

Aidan let out a long sigh. "This…faction? Is not as secretive as they think they are. Let's put it that way. But they attempt to be careful. And now that I've been brought into this situation, the others, who don't realize I know who they are, will attempt to remain under my radar. They won't be able to do that if they come after you or your brother again." She shrugged. "And I will let it be known that I gave my word you would be safe from threat unless you violated sanctuary on your own. Without a nudge. That should give you cover. For a few decades anyway."

Aidan grinned at that. And so did Agnes.

While Aidan's lifespan was nothing like Agnes's, Agnes actually didn't know exactly how old the hunter was. She looked mid-thirties, but she'd been around, her name whispered by demons, for decades already. Hunters could will a lot of things, including their own bodies to not age very fast. And Aidan had a very strong will.

"Winston is safe?" Jessica asked.

"And so are you," Aidan said, "as much as you can be." She raised her brows at Charles.

"I've no intention of violating my sanctuary," Charles said.

Which didn't precisely answer Aidan's unspoken question, but that was demons for you. Tricky, tricky.

"Since we're settled here," Charles said, "I'll just go let my brother know not to pack his bags. So to speak."

Charles stood and held a hand out for Jessica to proceed him. He stopped at the counter on the way out and paid for Agnes's and Aidan's drinks. Which Agnes thought only right since he'd dragged her into all this without any warning.

But to be fair, it had been a very enlightening and entertaining interlude.

Once the demon and his brother's lover had left, Aidan turned to face Agnes. "Thank you for serving as impartial judge. I'm sure we would have come to an understanding without a fight anyway. But he was less…aggressive about the whole thing with you here."

"You knew?" Agnes asked, smiling up at Nina as she gave Agnes a fresh cup of tea and set another class of Coke down for Aidan.

Aidan waited until Nina had left before saying, "I suspected."

"Hmm. Will this be a problem for you going forward?"

Aidan glanced toward the bookstore and pulled in a deep breath. "For me? Not in the way you think. But it is going to make the next couple of years…interesting."

"Oh good. One wouldn't want to get bored." Agnes raised her cup in a little solute.

Aidan followed suit with her own glass, finishing her drink before bidding Agnes goodbye and wandering into the bookstore.

Agnes went back to reading her book and sipping her excellent tea. Content with her day's entertainment. Happily returning to her peace.

FRANK AT THE CAFÉ

FRANK

Frank stared at the glass door of the café from his seat at the back of the room, watching people pass on the sidewalk. Watching people move in and out of the adjoining bookstore. Watching the nice woman behind the counter serve up delicious smelling mugs the size of small bowls filled with coffee of various types and the occasional cup of tea. Watching her giant Maine coon cat lounge on a stool he was clearly too large for, mostly ignoring the people coming and going from the coffee shop. Watched the older woman with her ever-present mug of tea reading something that looked suspiciously like erotica.

Watching his entire life and career go down the toilet.

He was never going to write again.

He'd never felt like this before. Hollowed out. No stories inside. Nothing he could glom onto and turn into a ripping adventure in fiction. Nothing. No sparks at all.

This was the first time in his forty-three years he just didn't want to write.

They called it burnout. He supposed he was. Lot going on in life. New teaching job at a school that was rougher than his last. Lot to learn. A new principal who didn't like him very much. Agent just dropped him, which meant he had to find a new one. Editor crawling down his neck looking for his next crime novel. The sales on his last book still earning out the advance, so no new money coming in from that direction until he turned in a new book. And the advance from that last book had been spent a long time ago.

If not for his day job, he'd be screwed. But the combination of day job, family life—a strained marriage and two small children to ensure had health insurance and food and a roof overhead—and the pressures of all the promotion his publisher wanted him to do, and he was just…

Tired. He was very very tired.

His husband kind of understood, but he was super busy with work, too. Work that earned more than Frank's two jobs combined. Work that meant they could keep the twins in a good, safe daycare—a place the twins loved going, so dropping them off in the mornings wasn't horrible. Or was less horrible anyway.

He and Greg had discussed Frank just quitting the teaching job, going full time as a writer. Their insurance through Greg's job was enough for the family. They'd manage with less.

But his writing income was so sporadic and unpredictable. And only came in, maybe, a couple of times a year. It wasn't anything he could count on. They could count on. Which meant he'd almost be better off giving up the writing.

The first time he'd had that thought he'd been swift and brutal about shutting it down. He didn't *want* to stop writing. He loved writing. This had been his life since…well forever. He couldn't remember a time when he had *not* made up stories.

But then the pressures of everything started to weigh more heavily. Moving schools. Difficult principal. The twins hitting a more complicated age. Hints that Jeromy might not be hitting all the age-appropriate milestones and suggestions they get him evaluated for autism. Greg's mother getting sick and needing to be settled in a nursing home. Greg's brother and sister not helping much with that process.

And then Frank's agent started pressuring him to write in the latest trendy genre under a new author name—but Frank only occasionally read romance and hadn't read any fantasy at all for years. He didn't *understand* this trendy genre on a bone deep level the way he understood mystery and crime fiction. He'd tried. And he'd failed. No one wanted his attempt at writing something it turned out he didn't enjoy writing. That was better for everyone in the end. Trying to write that book had been like pulling teeth.

But it had been the last straw for his agent. Who'd dropped him unceremoniously in an email that read more like a form rejection letter than an end to a years-long business relationship.

Everything felt like it was falling apart.

Then this…numbness. This lack of desire to write anything at all. No stories lurking in the shadows, popping their heads up when he was in the shower or putting dishes in the dishwasher. No stories traveling with him on his commutes. No stories filling his mind at all. They just weren't there anymore.

The internet suggested he get more sleep and take care of himself, eat better, drink more water, get more exercise. Touch grass. He was sure all that probably would help with the burnout. It made sense. Might be his only way back.

But with his editor breathing down his neck, he wanted to get this one last novel written, one last book turned in before he turned his attention to fixing himself.

It was just…there was no story there for the novel.

In desperation, while school was out for a long break, he'd stumbled across this coffee shop he'd never seen before. Attached to one of his favorite bookstores. He'd felt like the very clichést of clichés, but he had to do something. Writers wrote in coffee shops sometimes, right? Maybe the change of scenery, the people-watching, the smell of books just next door, would all spark some of that old creativity. Open up the part of himself that had shut down.

He'd been coming into the café for three days now. And nothing.

He was never going to write again.

At least the coffee was good. And the pastries were delicious. The croissants in particular. Didn't really qualify as "eating better" but there was something about the buttery goodness that did settle him and left him feeling peaceful. A moment of enjoyment when he first settled into his seat at the back of the coffee shop.

The delicious food and drink hadn't lured his muse back yet, though.

And today seemed like it would be another day of good coffee and croissants and no words. He'd have to give up. Might have to give up entirely. Admit to his editor there would be no book coming. And then figure out if he could fix his brain and ever write again, or if this was just…the end.

The Maine coon who had done little but sprawl across that stool by the register suddenly leapt down, revealing a surprising amount of dexterity for an animal roughly the size of a basset hound, and ambled over toward Frank. Frank liked cats, but he was more of a dog person. He had had a friend tell him that Maine coons were the dogs of the cat world, so as the Maine coon wove through the tables, Frank wondered if that was the case. The cat was certainly large enough to qualify as a dog, with lush, fluffy gray fur and pale blue eyes that were bright enough Frank could see the color halfway across the room.

The cat walked past the older woman drinking tea and reading erotica, and the two seemed to exchange a nod in passing. Which was strange. Then the cat walked up to Frank, bumped his large head against Frank's calf, and when Frank just sat there staring down at the cat, bumped him again.

Oh. That was probably a sign to give scratches, right? He lowered his hand slowly so the cat could move away if it didn't want scritches, but the cat dipped its head directly into

Frank's hand, so Frank obliged. He smiled at the animal as it began to purr, loudly. That sound was very soothing. He could sort of see why people got cats. Something about that soft fur and the rumbling purr seemed to quiet his mind. Left him in a bubble of peace. Bit like his first sip of coffee and that first bite of croissant. A moment to rest and savor. Just long enough to turn his brain off for a few seconds.

After a time, which Frank surprisingly couldn't judge, the cat nudged his leg again. And then wandered off, back to its stool.

Frank smiled. Guess the cat just wanted a scritch and his human was too busy filling orders. Fair enough. Frank was happy to obliged.

He looked at his plate and discovered he hadn't finished his croissant, which was surprising. He thought he'd taken the last bite. He still had more coffee than he remembered, too. So he took the moments of peace he'd found with the cat and stretched them out, after giving his hands a quick Purell, by eating the last bite of pastry slowly and sipping the remains of his coffee. He didn't try to think or invent or come up with a story in those moments. He just took the peace and quiet of eating and drinking.

At the very least, this new café gave him that.

When he was finished, he decided he should just go home. Maybe pick the twins up early and spend the afternoon watching *them* invent stories. He was about to close his laptop, the page in his word processing program still decidedly blank, when the bell over the door rang. And in walked a woman who caught his full attention.

She was like something directly out of an old Hitchcock film, but with a modern twist. Her dark brown hair was sleeked back into a sophisticated French twist, her wide-legged tan pants and button up, rose-colored silk shirt reminded him of something Katherine Hepburn would wear. Her heels were low and shiny. Her purse hung on her shoulder by a thin gold chain. And her makeup was impeccable. She looked like she'd walked out of one of his books, poised to torment the hapless private investigator while he solved the mystery of her murdered husband, a murder she was accused of.

Frank watched the story play out in his head. As she strode up to the counter, her gaze traveled over the patrons, lingering on no one, her expression closed but haughty at the same time. Her nails were perfectly manicured, polished in a soft pink, the perfection on full display as she tapped them on the counter, waiting restlessly.

She glanced toward the front door multiple times, like she was waiting for someone.

Frank reopened his computer, using it as cover so he could study the woman without appearing to stare. He started typing.

The barista had gotten her name for the order, even though she was the only one at the counter. Her name was Claudia. A good name for a femme fatale, he thought. Claudia… Probably something interesting but straightforward. Nothing French or fancy. Claudia Green. Yes. Probably something like that. Claudia Green. No

Greene, with an e on the end. He had no idea why, but that seemed to fit. Claudia Greene.

Here to meet someone. Her lawyer? Her lawyer. A man she had wrapped around her little finger. The man who was supposed to be helping her get out of her loveless marriage. Rich husband. Very rich. Very well connected. And scrupulously faithful, much to Claudia's chagrin. If he'd cheated, if he'd been cruel to her or hit her, she'd have cause. The divorce would be quick, and she'd get the money she was owed.

But, of course, Benedict had never cheated. Never hit her. Never even raised his voice to her.

Never given her anything at all she could use to take his money and leave.

She supposed she could still leave. People left their husbands all the time. But if she left, she left with nothing. All these years, all this effort. And to get nothing from it? Intolerable. She'd put up with his sweaty hands and bad breath and indifference for so long now. She *deserved* something for all that.

And it wasn't as if Benedict hadn't known what their marriage would be. That was in the contract. That was part of it all…

A man walked into the café then. Tall, young, handsome. Black hair and small glasses on a classically chiseled face. He wore a black suit and dark green tie, everything nice but off the rack and barely tailored to fit his wide shoulders. He was the kind of man others noticed, but he wasn't aware of that. He pushed his glasses up his nose and hunted the café, blinking a few times before he spotted her.

She hadn't taken him to bed yet. That would ruin everything. But she fully intended on taking him to her bed the minute the divorce was finalized. She was a little desperate to see if the hints she got of his body through his cheap but tailored suits would prove a match for her imagination.

But no sex until the ink was dry on her divorce, and her half of Benedict's money had moved into her account.

If she could manage all that.

Murder would be easier.

Claudia and her lawyer settled at a table to one side of the café, away from the front windows as well as the large, open entrance into the bookstore. They had things to discuss and she didn't want anyone to overhear them. But she also didn't want any of Benedict's associates to randomly walk past and spot her talking with a handsome young man. Then she'd have to explain he was her lawyer. And that would start questions she wasn't ready to answer yet.

They'd barely settled when her lawyer leaned across the table and whispered, "I received some news this morning and you're not going to like it."

She tightened her hold on her coffee mug, the big bowl shape large enough to take the pressure without crumbling. "What's happened?"

"Your husband is looking to file for divorce. Within the week. I only got the heads up because I'm…acquainted with one of the paralegals in his office. They warned me."

She didn't tighten her hands more, and she didn't react to his "acquaintance" comment. The news about her husband filing for divorce was so bad that what she really wanted to do was throw the mug through the front glass windows and scream until her throat hurt.

She didn't do any of that either.

"He doesn't have cause," she said through her teeth. That was the problem with her divorce filing, why they'd delayed so long. The prenup was very specific. And had contingencies to keep her safe from him just randomly dropping her without cause and leaving her with nothing.

The only way she could file for divorce and get anything was for him to give her cause—by cheating or hitting her or some other egregious act. The only way *he* could file for divorce and keep all his money was by having cause against her—if she cheated or hit him or some other egregious act.

Except that she very purposefully had done nothing egregious so that she could get her money.

"What. Cause?" She gritted her teeth as her lawyer adjusted his glasses and shifted around uncomfortably in his seat.

"Claims of infidelity. My paralegal acquaintance says there are photographs but they haven't seen them."

"There can be no photos. I haven't cheated." But if her husband had hired someone to impersonate her for pictures… or had some digital fakes created…

Oh. She was going to kill him.

She looked at her lawyer. "If he files before I do, we're screwed."

He nodded.

"Then we don't have any choice."

"We don't have cause yet for filing your divorce first."

"I'm not talking about divorce."

Frank blinked and looked at his computer screen. Story. There was actually a story there. Words. On the screen. It was rough. He needed a name for the lawyer. Maybe change Claudia's last name. He still wasn't set on that. And was the lawyer's paralegal a man or woman or nonbinary? Frank might change that, too. He had to flesh a lot of this out still. But…

He was writing.

He blinked a few more times and looked at the beautiful woman still standing at the counter, taking her to-go cup from the barista. Her gaze swept the coffee shop and then settled on him. She raised an elegant eyebrow, almost a question, and Frank found himself nodding, though he wasn't entirely sure why.

Almost in his head he heard her asking, "Did that help?"

And his answer was, "Yes."

She winked, her smile growing. Then she tapped the counter, said thank you to the barista, and headed out the door.

The giant Maine coon watched the woman go, then rearranged himself on the stool again, curling up in a ball so tight, Frank wouldn't have thought it possible of an animal so large.

The barista walked over, carrying a refill on his coffee. Frank glanced down. He'd forgotten he'd finished his drink.

He'd done that right before the woman walked in, hadn't he?

"Want another croissant, too?" the barista asked.

He didn't remember ordering the refill on coffee even, but he did like to ensure he paid for his time in the café by ordering regular hourly coffees, so maybe she'd just anticipated him. "No thank you," he said. He looked back at his screen. "I'm writing." This he said to himself, his voice awed.

At the back of his mind, he still felt the exhaustion that had led to the burnout. He knew he couldn't afford to ignore that or this one moment of inspiration would do him no good. But he was writing. He just needed to also rest and eat and sleep and play. If he did all the right things, took care of himself, maybe this start, this kernel, could be the next book. Get his editor off his back. Open up his storytelling muse again.

He wasn't sure. This hadn't fixed the exhaustion or the burnout. But...he did feel energy again. And he was excited about the possibilities of this story start.

He *wanted* to write more.

The barista smiled at him. "Glad to see the words are flowing. Sometimes you just need a muse, right?"

He startled and glanced up at her. She winked too, then returned to the counter, saying something he couldn't hear to the cat as she passed it.

Frank looked at the sidewalk outside the coffee shop again, where the woman with the slick hair and stylish clothing had disappeared into the crowds.

Muse.

Huh. She really had been.

The story crowded into his head again, so he took a sip of his coffee and started writing. The story bones fell out of his fingertips. He almost couldn't stop writing when it was time to leave. But when he did finally stand up and stretch his sore back and forearms—he'd forgotten to stand and stretch as often as he was supposed to—he looked at the pages he'd managed, the word count at the bottom of his writing program.

All those words. Something to work with tomorrow.

He smiled. Muse indeed.

BETTY AND AL AT
THE CAFÉ

BETTY AND AL

Betty hadn't seen Alexandra Mason for almost three years and she still wasn't prepared for the accidental encounter at the bookstore. She'd have thought, after all this time, things would be easier. She'd be able to greet Al with a kind of friendly former acquaintance sort of wave and then move on with her life, especially since Al had moved on with hers.

But no. That wasn't how Betty reacted. Her first reaction was to turn into a blubbering, awkwardly stammering dork. Of course. She'd never been able to be cool around Al. Not that she was cool normally. Normally, she wasn't quite this awkward, though.

"Hey. Hi. Wow. It's you," she stammered when she quite literally bumped into Al in the science fiction aisle as she was heading toward the romance section. "Good to, uhm, to see you?"

Al glanced up, blinked a few times, and her smile grew. "Hey! It's Beatrice Green. How are you, Beatrice Green?"

A weird laugh that sounded forced escaped from her. "Great, great. Thanks." Knowing Al remembered her full name was as disconcerting as coming face-to-face with her after all these years. "You?"

Al turned to face her fully, holding a paperback against her chest as she smiled. The smile made everything in Betty tight and jittery.

Around them, the bookstore bustled with people, all quietly perusing the stacks, lingering over a hardback at one of the display tables, scanning spines on higher shelves. Since it was a Saturday, things were pretty busy, but not so crowded you couldn't get near the shelves or pass people in the aisle. Just tight enough, though, Betty hadn't been paying close enough attention to *not* bump into anyone. That it was someone she knew was probably the worst coincidence.

The smell of coffee from the attached café had had Betty considering adding a stop next door to savor her rare afternoon off. At least, she'd been considering that before seeing Al again. Now, she couldn't think past the next moment and might have forgotten what coffee was.

"You still with the orchestra?" Al asked, completely ignoring Betty's question.

"Yup." She winced. What was she, twelve? "I mean. Yes. Yes, still with the orchestra."

"You made first chair yet?"

That Al remembered so many details about her was

overwhelming. And for an instant, Betty thought maybe the attraction hadn't been entirely one way back then.

Until she remembered that Al was like this with everyone. It's what made her such a great producer. She literally remembered everyone, their names, their families, their hobbies. And she'd certainly have remembered the line up of the city's orchestra from a time when she'd been producing a documentary about them. That documentary had won Al a prestigious award, and ensured the orchestra had sold out the next two seasons.

Betty rolled her lips into her mouth to keep another wince at bay, realized she couldn't speak like that, and said, "I did. Last year."

"Congratulations!" Al gave her shoulder a light thump that turned into a pat. Betty tried not to swoon. "I knew you would. You were the best cellist there, and everyone knew it."

That wasn't strictly true. The woman who'd been the first chair when Al had done the documentary was a legend. The only reason Betty moved up was because Gretchen had retired. But it was still a nice compliment, which, unfortunately, made Betty blush.

"How about you?" she asked, to get the focus off her because she knew Al would spot the blush and didn't want to talk about it. "You were on your way to Hollywood the last time we all saw you. Brand new big job." And since that took Al far away, Betty had swallowed her crush and pretended like it didn't break her heart just a little to see Al leave for good.

"Busy," Al said, with a little sigh. "But things are good." She brushed her fingers through her short blond-gray hair, the gesture ruffling the softness layers.

Al was only a few years older than Betty, but she'd had that blond-gray hair even three years ago. She'd worn it longer then, in a bob that brushed her shoulders. Betty found she liked this shorter style even better. It gave Al's wide face a sort of…she wasn't sure how to say it. A kind of sassiness? That sounded weird, didn't it? Al was tanner now than she'd been three years ago, her gray eyes bright, very faint lines creasing the edges when she smiled. And she still looked fit, though maybe a little underweight compared to last time they'd met.

She wondered if Al was taking care of herself? If she was getting enough to eat. Getting enough sleep. And then she wondered why she thought she had any right to consider telling Al go eat something and have a rest when they barely counted as acquaintances.

"Well, you look good," Betty said, then felt the heat of a blush crossing her cheeks again. Panic had her wanting to run away. And also not move in case Al disappeared. And also a little worried this was all some fever dream brought on by her perpetual state of being a singleton.

"Thanks," Al said softly. "You look good, too. Though, you always did."

"I…" She had no idea what to say to that. She latched on to another topic of conversation fast, before she embarrassed herself by saying something inane like, "really? You really think I look good?" Instead, she said, "That book looks interesting." And nodded to the book in Al's hands.

Al glanced down at it. "Ah. This. Yeah. Just…doing some research." She chuckled. "I've been roped into co-producing a science fiction TV series pilot and I'm not sure I'm up to the task."

"Oh, I bet you'll be great at that. You're such an excellent producer." Was she being weirdly fawning? Probably. "Do you not want to do the show?"

"No, I want to. It's a fun project. With a few actors I really want to work with." She waved her hand. "But you know. Always a little scary to try something completely new and different, right?

"Yeah. I get that. I was terrified the night I took first chair."

"And then you received a standing ovation, right?"

Betty laughed. "Me? No. The orchestra, yes."

"I bet the ovation was for you."

Betty found herself grinning too wide. She couldn't seem to help it. She needed to stop grinning so wide, but her face wasn't responding to her panicked warnings that she probably looked like an idiot.

"We'll be filming here, by the way," Al said suddenly. "For the TV pilot. I should get tickets to your next concert. See how everyone is doing."

"That'd be great. We're sold out for the season, but I'm sure they'd arrange something for you. After all, you're the reason we're sold out."

"I just boosted your name. You all did the work." Al glanced toward the café, through a large open archway in the wall that separated the two businesses. "I don't suppose you have time for a coffee? Chance to catch up? I've missed… this place."

"The bookstore?" Betty asked.

Al chuckled. "No. This city." Her expression softened. "Everything here really."

Betty considered making an excuse. The thought of spending more time with Al flustered her and made a crush she'd thought long gone lurch back to life with a vengeance. She'd be better off making excuses and leaving.

Safer.

But Betty had spent a great deal of time trying to be safe. And what had that gotten her? If Gretchen hadn't retired, Betty was certain she would have quietly remained second chair, maybe let herself fade into the background of the orchestra, just to be safe. Trying to stay safe had ensured a lot of lonely Saturdays, no one to share her day with. She hid in her music, in practice, and then in books, so no one could hurt her.

And yet, she'd still gotten hurt over the years. Without even getting to experience the good part before the bad.

If she said yes to the coffee, and that was the only time she spent with Al after this, at least she'd have had a good conversation with an attractive woman on one of her Saturday afternoons. It was better than running away.

"Sure," she said. "I was thinking a coffee sounded good."

The café was busy when they passed through the archway after buying their books, most of the tables occupied. That sort of put a damper on the idea of sitting around and having a chat. But just as Betty was about to chicken out and call the whole thing off, a woman sitting at one of the central tables stood and gestured to her place.

"You need a seat?" she asked. "I'm just leaving." She tucked a well-read paperback under her arm, slipped her small purse over her shoulder and picked up a tea cup.

She was an older woman with a twinkly smile that made Betty think the woman was giving her a wink even though she didn't.

"Thanks," Al said, with a genuine smile. "Beatrice, you hold the table. I'll get the drinks. Soy latte, right?"

Betty blinked, shocked Al remembered her preferred coffee, and had to nod her response because she couldn't find words.

Al grinned and head to the counter, where a woman in a green apron was helping customers. Beside the register, on a stool that was much too small for it, a giant gray cat curled in a huge ball, snoozing contentedly.

The woman who'd given them her table wished Betty a lovely afternoon and wandered out the main door of the café, the little bell overhead tinkling. The woman behind the counter waved goodbye to the woman as she left, calling her

Agnes. Betty assumed that meant she was a regular at the café. Betty wasn't a regular anywhere. What would it be like to be a regular in a place like this, and have people know her well enough to wave goodbye as she left?

She thought she might like that.

Al chatted for a few minutes with the woman behind the counter before collecting their coffees and bringing them back to the small table Betty was holding. Betty tried very hard not to acknowledge her disappointed jealousy that Al was flirting with the barista. Maybe she hadn't been. Again, Al talked to everyone and learned everything about them—and remembered those details! She'd probably just been doing that.

It occurred to Betty she'd better settle her wayward crush instantly because otherwise this conversation was going to be even more awkward than she'd already been.

"So," she said, sipping her coffee. Then paused. "Wow. That's really good." She sipped again. "Really good."

Al chuckled. "What were you expecting?"

"I don't know. Normal coffee. Not something quite so delicious, I guess. No wonder the place is crowded."

"Her cat's name is Boo! Don't you love that. Boo! Like a ghost. And he's gray. Apparently, he has light blue eyes too, so he really looks like a ghost. But he didn't deign to wake up while I was standing there." She chuckled.

"A cat named Boo." Betty smiled. "I like that." She cleared her throat when eye contact with Al and their shared soft smiles went on too long. "How's your coffee?"

"Excellent." Al raised her mug. "Got a latte, too. But

regular milk. No offense, but soy milk tastes like milk that's gone off to me."

"No offense taken." She sipped her drink again. "Especially when this tastes so delicious I can't even be offended."

Al chuckled. "You look really good, Beatrice. Life must be treating you well."

Betty shrugged. "I don't know. It's been…fine. I guess. Good professionally." Thanks to Gretchen retiring. "It's life. I guess." She needed to shift gears. "California must be treating you well, too. You look great and…tan."

Al let loose a laugh loud enough to make a few people turn and look. She didn't seem to notice the attention or the one man who scowled. "Hard with so much sunshine not to pick up some color."

"Well, it suits you." Betty wanted to sink into the seat. She hadn't meant to say any of that. Too close to being an admission. "Are you seeing anyone? That must be tricky with how much you travel for work. Or do you not travel as much. Though, wait, you said you would be filming here. That's called 'on location,' right?"

Al's expression did something funny that Betty couldn't interpret, displayed emotions Betty couldn't read. "It is called 'on location.' It's only a pilot, so I'm just here for a few weeks to start. But if it gets picked up, I'll be here a lot. Months at a time." Al glanced around and sighed. "Missed this city," she murmured.

Betty didn't miss the fact that Al had avoided answering the question about seeing someone. Which would have been really helpful information for Betty so her ridiculous little heart didn't do somersaults and her gut stopped its dancing at the thought of Al being around for months at a time. It wasn't like they'd see each other. She'd be working. Al would be working. The pilot hadn't even been filmed, yet, nonetheless picked up for a full season. Betty really needed to get her head out of the clouds and back to reality.

And knowing if Al was in a relationship would help that a lot. Like, a lot lot.

"If you have to be here for months, will that be bad?" she asked. "Since you've got a whole life in California and everything. It must be hard to leave things behind. People behind."

She wanted to wince but hid it. She couldn't have been more obvious, or more ridiculous, if she tried. But here they were. If Al hadn't figured out she was awkward by now, Betty would be surprised.

"No one who wouldn't survive my absence," Al said after a few moments, her gaze settled on Betty's.

"I'm…sorry?" She wasn't sure what to say to that comment. She wasn't exactly sorry. Well, okay, she sort of was because the comment meant Betty's ridiculous hopes flared to life even stronger than before and that was bad. But also, Al looked strangely sad about not having someone who would miss her at home, and Al being sad made Betty sad. She wanted only good things for Al.

"I work too much," Al said. "It makes it hard to have nice things."

"I get that. I practice a lot. We travel sometimes. The

concerts are mostly at night and sometimes during the day during the season. It's a lot more work than people assume."

"I remember."

Betty released an awkward chuckle. "Right. Right. So yeah. I understand. It can be hard for…other people to accept a crazy schedule."

"What do you do when the season ends?" Al asked, leaning back in her seat, cradling her mug.

"Sleep."

Al laughed again.

Betty grinned. She liked Al's laugh.

"And practice of course. There's always practice. We still do occasional shows out of season. But most of the off season practice is learning new arrangements and testing new things for the next season, so… Really, it's never ending."

"You ever get a chance to take a vacation?"

"Sometimes." Betty mostly used those breaks to stay home and read. By herself. But she didn't mention that. "Mostly, just a lot of work, though. I mean, I don't mind. I love what I do."

"Me, too!" Al leaned forward now, her expression intent. "Sometimes doing what you love takes time. And travel. And…effort."

"Right? Without all the work, we wouldn't be able to stay at the top of our game."

"And it's not like I *never* take time off," Al said, resting her arms on the table, the mug between her palms. "I take time off."

"Of course you do."

"It's just, you know, some of this never ends so there are phone calls and things."

"Sure. Deals don't just stop because you happen to be on vacation." Betty frowned. "Though it is important to have some quiet time, right?" She winced. "I've been told I work too much. Even by other musicians. That I need to take more down time. Get a life."

"I keep hearing the 'get a life' line, too. What a crock."

The comment startled a laugh out of Betty. Loud and delighted. Before she realized how loud she'd been and muffled the chuckle.

"Don't do that," Al said quietly, grinning with her. "You're allowed to laugh loudly."

Betty nodded, still smiling. "Getting a life *is* a crock, though," she said. "I'd rather get a cat."

Al nodded. "Definitely a cat. Love dogs, but am not around enough for them."

"Do you like cats?"

"I do." She leaned back in her seat again. "So I guess since you haven't gotten a life yet, that means you're not seeing anyone?"

Betty swallowed a too hot gulp of latte to hide her surprise at the change of subject. "Nope. No. No. Not seeing anyone. You?" After all, Al had brought it up, even though she'd ignored the topic when Betty had brought it up.

"Not seeing anyone," Al said. "I was. She left."

"Oh. I'm so sorry."

Al shrugged. "She didn't know how to live with a workaholic. I suppose neither do I?"

"Meaning?"

"I'm not sure how to live with myself this way. It's kind of the reason I want this pilot to get picked up. It would give me a little stability. At least for a few months. I could take a breath."

"You can't breathe now?" It was Betty's turn to lean forward, her arms resting on the table.

"Not most days," Al said with a nod. "The hustle never ends."

"I'm not sure if I should say sorry to that. You obviously love your work. You're very good at it. So that's nothing to be sorry about. But you also sound…" She trailed off and shrugged.

"What?" Al asked, not defensively but with genuine curiosity. "What do I sound?"

"It's not really my place…"

"Go on. Don't hold back now."

"You sound sad."

"Ah. That." Al sipped her coffee. "Yeah. Well, not so much sad as…tired. I'm tired and a little resigned. But I don't like feeling resigned."

"Resigned to what?"

"Being so busy I miss something really good."

"If it's worthwhile, I'm sure you won't miss it. Whatever it is."

Al's soft smile made Betty's insides flutter again. For just a moment, she'd forgotten to hold up her guard. Now she was afraid Al had just seen right through her to her soul.

"Maybe," Al said after a moment. "I thought I was super

busy today. Here for work. And look what happened. I met you again."

Yeah. More fluttering. And also a very vague feeling that Al might actually be…flirting with her? That couldn't be possible. "So you aren't sorry I literally bumped into you and nearly knocked you down?"

"No. Not at all."

Silence stretched, for a long moment. The sort of long moment that made Betty a little breathless. She ducked her gaze first, looking into her mug, at the almost finished coffee. She didn't remember drinking so much. But once her coffee was done, she wouldn't have an excuse to sit here longer and talk.

And Al had said she was busy. The trip to the bookstore had been work related for her, so she probably had to get back to work of some kind.

"You want another?" she asked, despite herself, motioning to Al's mug. "My treat this time."

"Sure. I could do another. But no soy, please."

Betty chuckled as she went to the counter, trying not to wobble because her knees were a little weak seeing Al's mischievous grin.

They talked for another hour. And Betty kept expecting Al to say she had to go, had work to do, nice-to-see-you-let's-stay-in-touch pleasantries without exchanging ways to stay in touch. Actually, Betty wasn't sure if she wanted that last pleasantry or not. It might be more heartbreaking than if Al just thanked her and left without any pretend promises.

But Al showed no signs of being in a hurry or needing to leave. She kept asking Betty about herself, her life, like she was genuinely interested—and because Al usually was interested in other people, Betty tried *so hard* not to take that interest personally, not to read too much into it.

By the end of the hour, however, her crush had gone from a banked and quiet thing to a full-blown fire and she just knew she was going to get hurt. But during that delightful hour of easy conversation and learning so much about Al as a person, Betty really didn't care. She didn't even care that she was half in love with the woman by the end of the conversation.

Before that hour, Al had been…a story to her. The *idea* of her had been what Betty had been attracted to. She was successful and vibrant, beautiful in a relaxed, mature way, friendly, and good around people, confident. All things that drew Betty. But it was only after getting to know her so much better that she really *saw* Al, saw the sadness and the hustle and the struggle and the *humor*. The confidence wasn't feigned, she really was confident in her skills and her talents, but she was also humble enough to give lots of credit to the people she worked with. She was funny, and self-deprecating, and Betty could see how this woman ended up getting personal details and histories from the people she talked to because Betty herself felt drawn to tell Al everything.

The hour flew by. And Betty only realized so much time

had passed when Al's phone, which she'd left in the pocket of her light jacket, buzzed.

That sound brought them both out of the little bubble of private conversation and they both sat back from the table blinking. Betty only realized they'd been leaning on the table, leaning into each other when they sat back.

Al sighed when she looked at the phone. "Sorry. I have to take this."

"No, it's fine."

Al gave her an apologetic look and went to the café door, stepping out onto the crowded sidewalk to take her call.

Betty looked at the coffee mugs on the table between them. At some stage, the barista had come over and taken their old mugs, Betty had some vague memory of that, but she had been so focused on Al, she'd barely noticed.

A few minutes later, Al returned looking resigned. She plopped back down in the seat across from Betty and held her gaze for a very long time.

Betty wanted to fidget, her fingers picking at the soft material of her linen pants, as she waited for the bad news. For this lovely interlude to come to a final end.

"I have to go," Al said finally. "Meeting. Some problems to troubleshoot."

Betty straightened and forced a smile. "Of course. Sure. I've taken up too much of your time already."

"No. No. You couldn't do that." Al continued to stare at her, her eyes a little narrowed. Finally, she said, "I'd like to… do this again. See you again. I'm in town for the next two months for the pilot and some other business. Would you…"

"That'd be great!" Betty rolled her lips into her mouth, blushing and feeling silly but also… Brave. Al made her feel brave. In a way she usually wasn't. "Yeah. That would be great. You wanted to see the orchestra again, right? I can arrange something."

"Perfect. I'd love that, thank you. But also… Would you like to have dinner with me tomorrow night?"

"Yes. Yes. That would be… Lovely."

Al's smile was slow and knowing, and Betty felt that look run through her in a sparkle of warm bubbles. "Great. Do you have a phone?"

They exchanged numbers. When Al entered Betty's and she typed in the name Beatrice, Betty said, "Oh, you can call me Betty. Everyone does."

Al grinned. Laughed. And said, "You know that song?"

Betty blinked. "Oh. Oh yeah. The Paul Simon one?"

Al nodded. "So when you call me, you'll know what you can call me."

"I will. Al."

A nd she did. Betty called Al the next day. They called and texted and talked every day after that for months. Al came to watch the orchestra play regularly—the conductor loved Al and got her a season ticket. Betty actually got to see the set of the pilot—which got picked up. And they spent every spare minute together, including flying back and forth to each other's homes when they had to be separated for work.

And when they got married three years later, they played the Paul Simon song during the reception, dancing in each other's arms, grinning, and reminiscing about their fateful meeting that day, all those years ago, at the café.

CARRIE ANN AT THE CAFÉ

CARRIE ANN

Carrie Ann walked into the café, dripping wet from a bucketing rainy day and satisfied with her state of misery. In two days, she'd lost her job, her marriage, and her home. The drenching rain and cold felt perfectly appropriate for her mental state.

But the café had looked so warm and beckoning, she hadn't been able to resist. Attached to a cheerful bookstore, the café was an open, bright contrast to the gloomy wet city streets behind her. There weren't many people in the middle of a work day. An older woman sitting in the center of the café, sipping her drink as she read what looked like a book of erotic poetry. And in the back a man on a laptop, typing furiously, the mug and pastry beside his laptop going unnoticed. Another woman walked in from the bookstore as Carrie Ann stood in the doorway dripping water onto the polished wooden floor. She was around Carrie Ann's age, late twenties, and carrying a pile of books to the counter.

Carrie Ann looked longingly at the books, but she didn't dare go into the bookstore until she stopped dripping.

The barista behind the counter smiled at the woman with the books and proceeded to make her a cappuccino while an absolutely ginormous and very furry gray cat sprawled on a stool—which the creature did *not* fit on—next to the cash register, looking extremely uninterested in everything going on as it licked a foot clean.

After serving the woman with the books, the barista looked over at Carrie Ann and her expression dissolved into immediate sympathy. "Oh, you're drenched. Do you want a towel? I have one back here." She ducked into a small room behind the counter and reemerged with a couple of white kitchen towels.

Coming around the counter she handed them to Carrie Ann. The towels weren't large, but two of them was enough for Carrie Ann to wipe her face and arms off and squeeze some of the water out of her hair.

"Sorry to drip all over your floor," she said to the barista.

The woman waved that away. "That's what mops are for. What can I get you to drink? Something hot, right? I'll bring it to your table. Sit anywhere."

Carrie Ann started to wave off the offer of a drink. She wasn't sure she should be spending any of her money on fancy coffees at the moment. She'd managed to save a little, in the secret account her grandmother had told her to get on her wedding day, which Carrie Ann had sheepishly opened two days after the honeymoon. She'd never been so grateful to her grandmother's advice before in her life. It was the only money her soon to be ex-husband hadn't stolen because he hadn't known about it.

There was maybe enough there to get set up in a new apartment. Maybe enough to see her not starve until she found a new job. Maybe. If she could get an apartment without a job or a job without an apartment. Those were details she still had to work out. At the moment, all her brain seemed able for was wandering around in the rain, though.

And a hot coffee, a fancy cappuccino even, sounded so wonderful she almost cried just thinking about it. So she ordered one and took herself off to one of the seats near the front window, one of the few plastic ones in the place so she didn't have to worry about destroying one of the wooden seats or soaking one of the cushioned chairs.

She laid the damp towels on the chair under her anyway and settled in, surprised she wasn't shivering. It was freezing outside, even though it was late spring, and she had gone out without a coat because she hadn't been thinking clearly when she left her friend Joy's place that morning. She was currently sleeping on Joy's couch. But Joy had a job and so did her wife and they couldn't babysit Carrie Ann twenty-four hours a day. Carrie Ann had felt awkward just sitting on their couch watching gameshows while they were out. She'd decided she needed a walk. She hadn't bothered looking out the window to check the weather. And once she'd stepped out into the rain, she hadn't bothered to turn around and go back.

She had no idea how long she'd been walking in the rain,

shivering with cold and feeling miserable, before spotting the warm, bright windows of the café. It had to be at least lunch time by now given how many people passed on the street just outside. The smells of coffee and pastry made her stomach grumble. She hadn't been hungry in days, but suddenly the idea of a croissant with her fancy coffee sounded like heaven.

When the barista brought over her cappuccino, Carrie Ann asked if there happened to be any croissants.

The barista frowned and said, "Give me a minute." Disappeared behind the counter, and reemerged with a triumphant whoop, bringing Carrie Ann an absolutely huge croissant on a small white plate that barely held the pastry.

"Last one," the barista said. "Great timing."

"Thank you." Carrie Ann tried to reach into the pocket of her soaked jeans for her wallet—that and her cellphone were the only things she remembered to take with her when she left Joy's apartment—but the barista waved her off.

"You can pay after you're done and you've had a chance to dry off. Here's another towel. Let me know if you get cold. I can adjust the temperature."

"Thanks." Carrie Ann was afraid she might cry at the simple gestures of kindness from a stranger, so she ducked her head and dove into her food and drink.

She couldn't remember the last time she'd had food or a coffee that tasted so good and so deeply, warmly satisfying.

She ate quietly, staring out the window, absently sipping her fancy coffee. When she got to the bottom, the barista brought her over a second. When Carrie Ann tried to demure, the barista said, "This one's on the house. It'll help you warm up."

Carrie Ann was already warm. Surprisingly so. The temperature inside the coffee shop was almost balmy compared to outside. But the second coffee made her feel even cozier. Her insides felt comfortably toasty instead of shivery, like she'd been sitting inside a sauna instead of walking in freezing rain.

More people started to trickle in and out of the café from the street and the adjoining bookstore. Carrie Ann was aware of the comings and goings, but most of her attention remained outside the window, her brain quiet but in a content way, not the numb, unable to process way that had shut her down for the last few days. A contentedness that felt like a reprieve.

When she finished the second coffee and set the mug down, she continued to stare out the window for a time, reluctant to leave. It was still raining, still cold outside. It wasn't cold in here. And her brain hadn't been spinning in circles of devastation. Just sitting and people watching and not worrying, even for this brief moment, felt so good she didn't want to let that go.

She reached for her mug, intending on returning it to the counter and paying for her food, only to find the drink was full again. She frowned and glanced around. The barista was busily working behind the counter, three people were in line at the register, and as far as Carrie Ann had seen, the barista was the only person working. She hadn't seen anyone walk up to her table, and while she might be a bit zoned out, she was certain she would have noticed someone trading out her coffee.

She frowned at the cup. It wasn't completely full. It looked like she'd sipped at it already. Maybe she hadn't finished her last mug after all, just thought she had because she wasn't really paying attention.

Taking a tentative sip, it tasted as delicious as what she'd already been drinking, and not too hot so it wasn't right from the espresso machine. Obviously, the coffee had been sitting there already, and she'd just been mistaken about having finished the full cup.

Silly. But at least she now had an excuse to continue sitting here for a bit longer.

At some point in her musings, the giant cat had wandered over and was now sitting in the chair across the table from her, not paying her any attention, just curled up on the unused seat at her table, sleeping. His soft purring rumbled quietly and provided a nice soothing accompaniment to the other cup clinks and conversations and the whirring of the espresso machine.

Glancing around, she realized the man at the back of the café was still pounding away at his computer, but the older woman with the erotic poetry book had left. There was at least half a dozen more people scattered around the various tables now, a couple of teenagers with their heads together over one's phone, a woman with a laptop tapping away much less frantically than the man in the back, an older couple exchanging books from a pile on the table between them.

The older couple left her feeling a bit misty eyed. She'd

assumed, on her wedding day, that's what her life would be like. Growing old with her husband, sitting in coffee shops after they retired talking about books and maybe planning their next trip to somewhere fun and exotic. She hadn't expected her marriage to last less than five years. She certainly hadn't expected her entire life to explode before she reached thirty.

And yet even those sad thoughts, the things that had kept her numb and tired and too miserable to even notice how wet and cold she'd been getting on her walk, none of that seemed to drop her back into the numb misery she'd walked in with. Just a little sad for what could have been, what should have been.

Instead of that, she had this now. Whatever *this* was.

She glanced down at her coffee, the mug still half full surprisingly, the foam on the top still fluffy and fresh.

What was *this* now?

A couch to sleep on for the moment and friends who wouldn't let her go homeless. Enough experience as a bookkeeper that she knew she'd eventually find a job. A place to live… Maybe somewhere nearby. This was a nice neighborhood. She wouldn't mind having a bookstore and coffee shop within walking distance. She had the nest egg her grandmother had advised her to save, so she wasn't broke. And she was rid of a man who, in hindsight, really hadn't ever liked her very much or treated her particularly kindly.

Since walking into this café, she'd been treated with nothing but kindness. And lovely coffee. And warmth. And a really excellent croissant. Her stomach was no longer churning acid. In fact, she thought she might get another pastry. And her numbness had melted away, leaving her sad, even melancholy, but…

Surprisingly okay.

Whatever *this* was inside this little beacon of light and warmth and delicious smells, she was grateful for it. Grateful for the giant gray cat's steady purring, and the hot foamy cappuccinos and the delicious food and the man pounding his keyboard in the back and the barista with the towels and the quiet hum of noise and movement between the café and the bookstore.

She was grateful for finding this place. She'd never seen it before. Hadn't even known the bookstore was here. But having found it, the place felt like somewhere she'd always come, someplace she felt comfortable. A home-away-from-home where she could get her thoughts together without feeling overwhelmed.

She'd definitely be coming back more. Frequently.

Though, next time, maybe a little less wet.

JOAN OF KERRY AT
THE CAFÉ

JOAN

Joan went into the bookstore first. She wanted to ensure the little bugger hadn't snuck in there and hidden behind one of the shelves after going through the café's front door. From dragon back, watching him sneak into the café had been easy, at least for Rory since dragon eyesight was excellent. Joan was getting to the stage where she might need reading glasses. But that was a different story.

Rory had definitely seen the little bastard go in through the café entrance. But the bookstore and coffee shop were connected, and it would have been very easy for Harold to sneak out the bookstore the minute Joan stepped into the café.

Because Rory was a dragon and needed to keep a low profile—which meant not being seen by humans because that would lead to chaos—he'd dropped Joan on the roof across the street before taking flight again to make sure Harold didn't sneak out while she was getting down to street level.

Fortunately, while she couldn't talk into Rory's head, mores the pity, he could speak into hers, so even while she was down here, he'd be able to communicate with her. The trick was that she couldn't communicate with him while inside. Rory had excellent hearing, but even that was limited by the noise inside human buildings.

He had confirmed no sign of Harold sneaking out before Joan reached the bookstore door, though, so she knew the little bugger was in there somewhere.

She'd left her sword with Rory so she could blend in betterer. Her normal clothes were ordinary enough—cargo pants and a zip up fleece—but a long sword resting on her back did tend elicit a few gasps.

And she needed to accomplish this without drawing too much attention.

She stalked through the bookstore, checking behind the back shelves and searching every nook before heading toward the café. Harold was a sneaky little gobshite, and she wouldn't put it past him to hide in the smallest corner of the bookstore.

By the time she reached the café, though, Harold was sitting at a table, sipping on a mug of coffee that looked huge in his small hands.

The goblin was one of the uglier ones—in goblin terms—and so could almost pass as human. Shorter than an average human child, but with an older face and wide shoulders. He was also a more ordinary shade of brown, something a human might actually have. Goblin green would never have blended in. His had few warts or bumps on his face, his nose was crooked but just looked like it had been broken once or twice, he only had two eyes, and his black hair and beard were curly and short. His eyes were a bright bright green, but unless someone nearby looked closely, the strangely bright color wouldn't be too noticeable.

Harold passed as a human with dwarfism in the human world. And because humans were awkward, they often looked past him in their attempts not to stare. His fellow goblins might consider him extra ugly in a bad way—there was ugly in a good way among goblins, but Harold wasn't it —but Harold was one of the few who could walk in the human world without immediately raising alarms.

The human world had long ago stopped believing in fairies and monsters and dragons for that matter. So the Fae stayed in Faery, the dragons who were awake stayed hidden, and the monsters… Well, that's where Joan came in. She and Rory took care of monsters. Some of them anyway. The really ancient ones. There were others who went after the ordinary day-to-day monsters.

Right now, though, she was more concerned with one particular, pain in the arse goblin, who'd gone and stolen a golden scale from her dragon companion. A golden scale that was worth way too much in the goblin world and would only cause trouble if Harold got it there. Also, Rory did not appreciate having his scales stolen.

Harold looked up as she approached, his mouth twitching under his beard. Most goblins didn't do the full beard and mustache the way Harold did. She thought he might do it to hide how human he looked, but honestly, it just made him look more human.

"I'm here for the scale, Harold," she said. "You should know better."

"Sit," he said, his voice higher than one might expect looking at him. "Please."

The please made Joan frown. Goblins didn't "please and thank you" often. Goblin society had different rules for politeness. She looked around the café, noting the number of people sitting at the scattered wooden tables. No one was paying her and Harold any attention. Behind the counter, a young woman wiped down the espresso machine. And next to the cash register a giant Maine coon sprawled on a tall stool that was obviously too small for him. The cat didn't seem to notice.

Neither the cat nor the woman behind the counter paid her any attention either. So. She glanced down at Harold. Then took the seat opposite him. This put her back to the door, but she had a dragon keeping guard outside, so if any more goblins tried to sneak up on her from behind, she'd have more than enough warning.

"Scale, Harold," she said. "Now. I won't ask again."

"You didn't bring your sword inside?"

"I don't need it for you."

"Hard to be yerself in the human world, inn'it?"

"No. I'm myself right now. Just without a sword." She held his gaze.

Harold shifted uncomfortably in his seat. Then slid

something across the table toward her. A golden dragon scale. The overhead café lights caught the scale's surface, making it glitter briefly before Joan put her hand over it and covered it. Couldn't be drawing attention to the thing in the middle of a human establishment.

"Want to explain why you risked Rory's wrath to steal one of these?" she asked quietly.

"To get you here. Needing yer help, aren't I?"

"Help?" Her frown deepened.

Goblins didn't come to her for help. She was usually the one stopping their plans. And she'd had some issues lately with the last few aspirants to the title of Goblin King. As far as she knew, the goblins were still working out their kingship issue and no one had filled the roll for longer than a few weeks before getting… Well, the goblins tended to be a bit vicious with fallen kings.

She was very curious what sort of help Harold could be asking for.

"Coffee?" The goblin raised his mug, which looked more like a soup bowl in his small hands. Another thing that made Harold stand out in the goblin realm but allowed him to blend in in the human realm. His hands were very human looking, if small for his size, with no standout breaks or warts or anything that might give him status among goblins.

"No thank you," she said to the offer of coffee.

"'S really good here."

"More of a tea drinker."

"Tea's good too, I hear."

"You hear? You come here often?"

"Me? Na. Just… No one notices me here when I do, so… Maybe. Yeah. Sometimes."

"Fair enough. Why are we here now?"

"Said it. Needing yer help."

"With?"

Harold set his mug down and leaned across the table toward her. No one was paying attention to them, so she wasn't sure why he felt the need to whisper, but she leaned in anyway, lowering her head so they were about on level.

Harold whispered, "They be wanting to make me king."

<hr>

Joan blinked. Then straightened in her seat. "They…"

"Want to make me king. Me!" Harold straightened too, his very green eyes blinking rapidly before he picked up his large mug in trembling hands. The hot liquid sloshed around but Harold didn't seem to notice. "King. Me! The very idea of it…"

"I…" Joan cleared her throat and tried again. "Why?"

"Obvious, aren't it. I'm the most horrible."

"You…aren't, though. And also, and I mean this respectfully, you're pretty timid. For a goblin king."

"Right, you are. I've been happy my whole life being in the corner and dark and no one paying me no mind. Not since I was a youngling. Lost interest in picking on me then, didn't they. Eventually. Been fine ever since. As it could be. Right. And me, I stayed out of the limelight. Nice and quiet and in the background and no one noticing me. Until last week.

When one of them bastards pointed at me and said, 'Make 'im the king.' And didn't everyone agree!"

"Huh." This was…unexpected.

"So," Joan began, then stopped. The whole idea was just so preposterous. Harold was the last possible goblin she would have ever thought of to be king. The kings were usually aggressive, violent, petulant, and ambitious. There were deadly competitions to become king.

And the prospective king had to present a very shiny and unique valuable of some kind, something that would impress the other goblins. No king became king without presenting the most unique shiny object. That was part of it all. Joan had gotten sucked into the chaos a few times before, once when the shiny object was a few of Rory's scales.

Since she was here because Harold had stolen one of Rory's scales, she supposed she wasn't completely surprised by this turn of events. But also, Harold had given her back the scale.

"Why did you steal a scale and then give it back?"

"Like I said, right. To get you here. I need ye to convince 'em all I'm never suited to being the king."

"I still don't understand why they randomly picked you."

"See, it's like this. All the others been killing each other, right? Just hacking away at our stability and making it hard to get back to goblin work, like stealing and corrupting kids and the like."

Joan narrowed her eyes.

Harold held his hands up. "Don't scowl at me. It's our job, inn'it? It's what goblins do. Anyway, with all the murdering of kings and such, no one's been able to do the actual work of goblining. Some bright spark decided I'd be a better option, seeing as how I've no interest in murdering anyone, and if they all get behind me, any usurpers will get killed before they make it to next Thursday, right? So now, they're all behind me, wanting me to be the king."

"And what makes you think they'll listen to me about *not* making you king?"

"They respect you, right? After that whole thing with the dragons and the Protector and all. They'll listen to you."

Joan sat back in her seat to consider the situation. In all honesty, the unrest among the goblins had been a constant background irritant for her for a while now. If they weren't stealing Rory's scales, they were unleashing monsters from the precious shiny objects they kept stealing.

Having some stability in the goblin realm would make her life easier.

And if all the goblins were prepared to get behind Harold as the king, then there was no possibility of any of them trying to kill him. That was the whole point, wasn't it? To stop all the infighting and just *have* a king.

A king who wasn't particularly ambitious or violent or aggressive. Maybe a little petulant, but in the circumstances, she could hardly blame him. Harold was quiet. He'd returned the scale he'd stolen, so she could trust him not to keep coming for Rory's scales. And he wasn't likely to go looking for unique shinys to keep the goblins in line and supporting him, because they already wanted him as king without all the bells and whistles. Not likely to unleash ancient monsters on accident. That was a real bonus.

She tilted her head to one side, studying the goblin. "Have you considered…accepting the job?"

"Wait!?!" His screech captured the attention of everyone in the café, all eyes turning to look at him. Harold scrunched down in his seat, trying to look invisible, and said more quietly, "Are ye daft? I've no business being king. They'll kill me for sure. Don't have the stomach for keeping all them goblins in line, do I?"

"But, Harold, they'll stay in line behind you because they've picked you. They want you to be their king. They won't support anyone trying to kill you or overthrow you. They want stability and a less ambitious option. That's you."

"Yeah, but…" Harold scowled and glanced around, as if the answers to this conundrum could be found in a neighbor's coffee. "But I'm no king. I'm just…me."

"I think that's the point."

"I think it is, too," Rory said, proving he'd been able to overhear this conversation the entire time and better than Joan had assumed.

"Rory agrees," Joan added for Harold, who wouldn't be able to hear him.

"The dragon thinks I'd be a good king?" Harold sounded so appalled Joan almost laughed. "I can't, don't you see. I don't know how."

"Harold, look, the goblins are obviously not looking for the same kind of king they've always had. They want someone different. You can be any kind of king you want and do it however you want. Stay in the corner doing your own thing and every so often look up and make a proclamation. Meanwhile, the rest of them can get on with being goblins." She narrowed her eyes. "So long as there is no corrupting or kidnapping children involved anymore. Not on my watch."

Harold frowned, tugged at his beard hard enough to make Joan wince. "But…" He paused, looked up at her. "You think?"

"I mean, it's up to you of course. I could still talk to the others and tell them you don't want the job. But they're as likely to listen to me as a goat. And I'd worry about them killing you for turning down the job."

His eyes widened again. "Hadn't thought of that. Wouldn't want to give offense."

"And once you were king, you could always make a proclamation that they aren't allowed to kill you."

"King can't make that kind of proclamation." He raised bushy brows. "Can they?"

She shrugged. "Don't see why not. You'd be the king."

"Would be nice not to worry all the time one of 'em takes it into their head to toss things at me anymore. Only one never gets nothing tossed at 'im is the king, right. And some of them tossed things are big. Would be nice not worrying about that anymore."

"Would," Joan said with a firm nod.

Harold straightened. "I could make a proclamation saying no more corrupting or kidnapping younglings, right. And then, then they'd still be allowed to corrupt and steal adults what need it. But no more children. I could do that."

"Would you do that?" The whole stealing kids and turning them into goblins was sort of the stock and trade of goblins, even if she disapproved greatly and made an effort to stop it when she could.

"Stealing kids in modern times is complicated anyway. Too many cameras and whatnot. Can't be giving those kids a good view of our treasures, right. The whole of everyone would descend on us, looking for treasures. Lot of adults what need stealing, no one cares they're gone. They make decent goblins eventually too, right. Better than some of them modern kids. Too modern. Like to insert modern ways." Harold wrinkled his barely broken nose at that idea.

"You do realize you'd be a 'modern way,' too, right?" Joan said, trying to suppress her grin. "No shiny or unique treasures to earn the title. No blood and murder and fighting to get it. Just...appointed by the others because they want you."

Harold looked aghast again, and Joan finally had to chuckle.

"It's okay, Harold. The modern part, we can keep between us."

"So." He swallowed so hard his beard bounced. "So you think. Maybe. I could be king. Without, like, dying?"

"I think you could. I think you might just be the perfect goblin king."

"Don't lay it on too thick," Rory said in her head.

Except she wasn't. She really did think Harold might just be the perfect king. One that could actually bring stability to the goblin realm finally.

"Okay. Okay. Well. I think. I think I better get back, inn'it. Get that whole crowning thing over with so I can make my first proclamations."

"Congratulations, King Harold."

"King Harold." He shook his head. "Who'd 'ave thought it."

"Just no stealing Rory's scales again, right? We can't be having that."

"No no. No more scales for me."

Harold scrambled up from his seat, gave a little tip of his head in solute, then hurried out the café door, looking both ways before scrambling off to the left.

Joan pushed herself to her feet and, after a moment, went to the counter for a cup of tea to go. She liked the vibe in this place. Comfortable and no one was too noisy. She still wouldn't bring her sword inside. But if the tea was good, maybe she'd come back.

Especially now that she didn't have to worry—at least for the immediate future—about the goblins.

The tea, as it happened, was very good.

MYRA AND CHRISTOPHER AT THE CAFÉ

MYRA AND CHRISTOPHER

The café's warm coziness wrapped around Myra the minute she pushed inside, the smell of coffee and pastries with just a background hint of books from the adjoining bookstore a delightful combination. Almost as delicious as Christopher's scent—whether he was oozing ordinary dragon shifter smells of leather and musk and a very faint hint of sulfur, or he'd started to smell like sugar cookies.

She really loved when he smelled like sugar cookies.

"I've been here before," she said over her shoulder to him as they stepped inside.

Christopher was a looming seven-foot-tall presence at her back, and the people filling more than half the tables in the café all turned at once to look. Hard not to at least glance up when a man of Christopher's stature walked into a room. He was so used to that reaction, he ignored it. And the café's patrons were so unbothered, they all went back to their various books and drinks and conversations, creating a quiet hum of background noise.

"Trust me," she said. "Coffee is excellent. And the owner and her cat are great."

"You know cats and I often have issues, right?" Christopher said, his voice deep and rumbly.

She loved his voice. "This cat's a little different. But also, I did not know that, and now I'm amused because I think of dragons and cats as being very similar."

"You do?" He looked so offended she wanted to laugh out loud.

"Sort of, yeah. Ungovernable. Independent. Likes to nap on large piles of stuff…"

He rolled his eyes, which did make her chuckle, and put a hand to her lower back to guide her to the counter, which made her tingle in a good way.

"Dragons are governable," he murmured, "or no one would pay attention to the king."

"Fair enough. And wouldn't that just piss your father off."

"It absolutely would."

At the counter, the owner stepped up to the register. A woman whose age was impossible to judge because she was a witch but who looked in her mid-thirties. As Myra recalled, her name was Nina. And the huge gray Maine coon curled up on a stool that was much too small for him next to the register was aptly named Boo. Myra supposed he was a little ghost-like in the way he moved around silently and was a pretty pale shade of gray—even his blue eyes were pale—but he was too fluffy and cute to be a ghost. He was also amenable to scritches around the head most days, so she gave him some as she placed her and Christopher's order.

Once they had their drinks and a blueberry muffin for her, they settled at a table near the back. The only person sitting nearby was a man so busy typing away at his laptop he ignored them. The rest of the patrons were too far away to overhear them—unless there were other shifters in the room, but Myra hadn't spotted any—so the table gave them a nice place to talk in private.

And to conduct their business.

"I'm not sure meeting this particular person in a place you like to visit is a good idea," Christopher murmured quietly.

"Afraid he'll ruin it for me?"

"Or be able to find you here too easily."

"I'm harder to find than that. Especially when I don't want to be."

"I find you," he said, though there was a rumble of innuendo in that statement.

He did always seem able to find her no matter where she was. A lot of that had to do with excellent dragon eyesight and a heightened sense of smell. But Myra had been practicing hiding from dragon shifters for months now and gotten much better at it.

She still couldn't hide from Christopher.

Not that she wanted to. In fact, she sort of enjoyed when he found her no matter where she was or what she was doing. So long as it didn't screw up the job she was attempting. And he was pretty good about being more helpful than harmful when she was working. Especially now that they were working together more.

"You're a special case," she said. "Remember I've been living in the same city with people who would *love* to find me and either turn me over to the police or kill me. And yet here I am, still doing my thing."

Her thing was stealing stuff. She was magically predisposed to it—meaning her magic was thief's magic. And she was very good at stealing things. Even without magic she had spent years honing her skills. In fact, stealing things was exactly what had gotten her in trouble with the dragon king in the first place. But since that led to her meeting Christopher, she had trouble thinking of that as one of her biggest life mistakes anymore—even if it had felt that way at the time. Still a mistake, because she'd gotten caught. But not one she regretted anymore.

Helped that the dragon king had laid off lately. Lot easier to date the dragon king's son when the dragon king wasn't trying to get you killed.

"Besides," she said, "this isn't the first time I've done business here. It'll be fine."

Christopher gave her a look.

She shrugged. "The owner is a witch. Things here run more smoothly than they might in another coffee shop. And people that aren't welcome tend to…forget about the place. I'm not saying bad people can't or don't walk in here. But I am saying they don't often come back once they do."

Christopher gave the woman behind the counter an

assessing look and then nodded. "Okay then. Why didn't you say so in the first place?"

"Honestly? I wasn't sure how you'd react to a witch."

"Her familiar should have been your bigger worry. Witches and dragons actually can get along."

"Hey, Boo didn't even yowl at you. He completely ignored you, in fact."

"He did, didn't he." Another of his assessing looks.

She nudged his shoulder. "Head back in the meeting."

She didn't want him to inadvertently cause trouble for Nina. Not that he ever would on purpose. He had a thing about damsels in distress and helping them even at a cost to himself—which was adorable and sweet actually—so she knew he wouldn't do anything to harm Nina or her business. His expression said he'd be interested in coming back here, though, maybe turning Nina into an ally. Which would be great on the one hand. Nina would be a good ally. But also, where Christopher went, so did his father, and Myra did *not* want the dragon king to know about this place.

Christopher glanced at her, his expression difficult to read, but then nodded and said, "When is he due?"

"Now." She nodded at the door as the bell over it chimed and a very ordinary looking human man walked in.

He was average height, brown hair, brown eyes, pale skin, dressed casually in jeans and a t-shirt under a zip-up hoodie with the hood down. His age was hard to judge, somewhere in his middle years, probably late-thirties, early-forties. He looked perfectly harmless. A good disguise for someone who was anything but harmless.

The man glanced around, spotted them, and started toward the back of the café. Paused, then returned to the counter to order a drink.

Hm. Myra would give him that. Better and smarter to be a good customer. Doing business in a place like this and not ordering was rude. Also, Myra liked that both Nina and Boo would be able to take his measure directly. That would ensure their safety later on.

It wasn't so much that Doug was dangerous himself, though he was. It was more the people he worked with, the people who counted on him to…clean things up. They were the dangerous ones, the stupid ones, the careless ones. They were the people who would hire someone like Doug to fix their mess so they never had to suffer, while the people they harmed were quietly taken care of. And not in a good way.

Doug didn't always eliminate people. Sometimes he blackmailed and bribed them to make them go away. Sometimes he did other negotiations or jobs to make a problem no longer a problem. Sometimes he did just quietly killed people. He wasn't particular about it and he wasn't emotional about it. He did his job, fixed problems for his clients, got paid well for it, and carried on with his life.

Under normal circumstances, Myra would never work with someone like Doug. She might end up one of Doug's targets—though so far, she'd managed to avoid that. She typically stole things from people who actually had so much they didn't realize the things she took were even missing. These days anyway. And sometimes she stole for good reasons—returning items to rightful owners, that kind of thing. Most of the time, though, it was just the challenge of the theft. More than the actual thing she stole, if it was a tough job, an *impossible* job, she found it hard to resist.

Which was what got her into trouble with the dragon king in the first place. Took a bet she shouldn't have. Live and learn.

At any rate, she'd managed to carry on with an entire lifetime of stealing without ever getting on the bad side of someone who would hire someone like Doug. So she wouldn't ordinarily go out of her way to meet with someone like Doug. Especially Doug in particular. His reputation proceeded him.

But in this particular situation, their goals actually aligned.

Doug gave Nina a casual smile and nod, he did not attempt to pet Boo—which Myra thought might be a good thing—and then he carried his hot mug across the café to join Myra and Christopher. Myra watched him approach but also flicked a glance at Nina. The witch was watching Doug, her eyes narrowed, and she murmured something to Boo.

Good. She'd clocked him. That ensured the people here would be safe should Doug ever come back for more nefarious reasons.

It occurred to Myra as Doug took his seat that having this meeting here might mean she got herself banned for bringing someone like Doug into the café. That would suck. But she'd understand. She'd still have arranged this meeting here. Because she knew it was the safest place around to do this.

Doug gave them each a nod. "Myra. Your highness."

Christopher flinched slightly and shook his head. "Christopher is fine."

Doug nodded again. Sipped his coffee.

There were no pictures of the royal family anywhere. Not on the internet, not with the press who absolutely adored everything dragon shifter. So Doug didn't know Christopher was one of the dragon king's sons because he'd seen a picture of him. He knew from some other time they'd encountered each other. Christopher hadn't come clean about that past meeting yet. But if she knew her dragon shifter prince, it probably had something to do with a damsel in distress, and Christopher was low level embarrassed to discuss it. He was such a softy. For a fire-breathing dragon.

"She says the heirloom is still with him," Doug said, getting right down to business. "Did something go wrong?"

Myra grinned. "You said she needed this done…quietly. Well, we did this quietly. And in a way that she'll have the satisfaction of getting her grandmother's heirloom back from her ex, while he'll never know it's missing, so he won't go to court or send someone to arrest her. Win-win as they say."

Doug took another sip of his coffee. Black. Dark. Smelled good and strong across the table. Myra preferred her sweet and milky coffee, but she appreciated a good black coffee.

"You have it then?" He looked so doubtful Myra was offended.

"Are you good at your job?" she asked.

"The best."

"Yeah. Well so am I."

"Then where is it?"

Christopher lifted the backpack he'd set under the table onto his lap, then went back to sipping his tea. He liked coffee but he tended toward tea when given a choice.

Doug's gaze flicked to the backpack. Then he stared at Myra. "I'm impressed."

"You should be."

The job hadn't been an easy one. Recovering the heirloom, which turned out to be a handmade wooden box with two silver chalices inside, had been complicated by the fact that Doug specified the ex-husband couldn't know the box was missing. That it would be dangerous to his client if the ex discovered the box gone.

That had, of course, hit Christopher right in his soft spot. Hit Myra, too. She might be picking up Christopher's penchant for wanting to rescue people. Little inconvenient, but not a first.

To keep the ex-husband in the dark, they'd had to get replicas made that would pass muster with the husband for… well, forever if necessary. Usually, when Myra put replicas in place, the fakes only had to pass for a few days, sometimes only a few hours. Just long enough for her to get the real object away and safely hidden or sold. The forgeries being discovered was usually part of the plan. The possessor of a "real" artifact or art piece typically wanted people to *know* it was real, and that was impossible if everyone still believed the "real" version was in a museum or gallery or someone else's collection.

People's egos—the people who bought stolen goods— were big, and they liked others to know what they had.

Myra didn't normally care about that part. She stole things for the challenge, and then either sold them, kept them, or replaced them a few weeks later. Depended on what she'd taken and why she'd taken it. Selling valuable items ensured she never had to worry about money, but it was also the more irritatingly complicated part of her career.

Until Christopher, Myra had never really worked for others. She stole what she wanted, when she wanted, for her own reasons. Then she worked with someone afterward to sell the loot.

Now, though, Christopher had decided to start helping people in more direct ways. Often those ways involved less than legal activities. And she was very good at the theft part of those activities. She still didn't consider that she was working for clients so much as she was working *with* Christopher. A technicality that she pretended made all the difference.

This had been one of those jobs were Christopher wanted to help the wife. A damsel in distress who just wanted her grandmother's heirloom back from a bastard of an ex. Doug was a middle man, the person the wife had originally hired. But because fixing her situation required some nuance and burglary skills, he'd turned to experts.

Doug nodded at the black backpack. "Can I see?"

Christopher opened the zip and tilted the bag so Doug could see inside. He didn't hand the bag to Doug, yet, though.

Doug nodded, his brows raised as he glanced at her. "Looks authentic. I can depend on this *not* being the replica?"

"You can." She smiled. "The wife will know the difference. There's a very tiny flaw worked into the real set of chalices that isn't in the replica. A sort of…artist signature that you'd have to know about to even notice. I had my guy leave that out. The ex doesn't know about the flaw. He won't spot the fake."

One of the most important parts of her job was the research. And because this job involved someone like Doug, she had researched the shit out of this case. Every single part of it.

"You're certain?"

"I'm certain." She leaned back in her seat, cradling her mug, waiting for Doug to decide if he believed her or not. He didn't trust her, of course. She wouldn't trust her either if she were Doug. Just like she didn't trust him. But they *were* both professionals.

"Fine." Doug pulled out his cellphone and punched in some things. He spent a few minutes, tapping at the screen, then nodded and looked up. "Money's been transferred. Your guy should be seeing it any moment.

They waited until Christopher's cellphone dinged. He checked the screen, also nodded, then handed the black backpack over to Doug without a word.

Their "guy" Jeffry would already be transferring the money to several different accounts so it couldn't be snatched back. They might require a certain level of professional trust here, but they also weren't stupid.

"My client will be delighted," Doug said. The bell over the door rang and Myra looked up.

To see the ex-husband walking into the café.

Christopher showed no outward sign of reacting to the husband walking into the café, but Myra felt him tense beside her. She stared hard at Doug as his real client walked toward them.

The ex-husband's name was Marshall Amato, and he was one of the wealthy assholes that Myra loved to steal from. The kind of careless mess of a human who never suffered consequences for his actions. His ex-wife, Una Thurgood, had been lucky to get out of the abusive marriage. But not lucky enough to get out with anything she'd brought into the marriage. Including her grandmother's heirloom. Amato had the lawyers, the money, and the connections to make her life shit if she didn't do as he wanted. The divorce had been her idea, but he'd dictated the terms. And left Una destitute.

Which was how Christopher and Myra knew she hadn't had the money to pay for someone like Doug.

That was also why they'd taken this job.

Amato stalked toward them in his crisp designer pants and polo shirt, looking like he'd just stepped off a yacht. Thick brown hair, sun-tanned skin, a narrow jaw and thick lips. Myra supposed he was probably handsome to some people. She found him slimy. He whipped off his designer sunglasses when he reached the table and sneered at them.

She raised her brows at the look. Christopher's expression never changed. He also didn't look up and acknowledge Amato. He and Doug were too busy having a staring contest.

So she took the lead with Amato. "Fancy seeing you here," she said with a grin and lifted her coffee mug. "You should get a drink if you're going to join us. Rude not to."

"Why the fuck would I care about that?" He sat next to Doug and took the black backpack when Doug handed it to him. He checked on the contents, then smirked at them. "You really think I wouldn't have noticed the swap?"

"No," Myra said. "I don't think you would have noticed the swap. If you hadn't arranged it."

Amato's left eye twitched.

"But what I'd like to know is, why? Why arrange to have something you already own stolen and frame your ex for it?"

"This was the only thing from the marriage she wanted. And it's mine. She can't have it."

"That…doesn't answer my question."

"And I'm not going to either."

"I will, then," Christopher said, though he was still staring at Doug. "You suspected the wife you left destitute had hired someone to retrieve her heirloom. You went to Doug to fix the problem once and for all. But you wanted to see if the theft could actually be carried out first. Because you're arrogant and an idiot."

Amato started to rise at that insult. Doug set a hand to his arm and the man settled. Doug and Christopher had not once stopped staring at each other through this.

"You were even willing to pretend to pay us, to make it look like all this was on the up and up. You intended on holding the failure over your ex-wife's head as Doug killed her. A little salt in the wounds for her betrayal. Because she left you and no one leaves you, right, Marshall? No one betrays *you*."

Christopher's voice remained even during the recitation. Amato, on the other hand, got redder and redder and he looked like he was about to explode. Myra sipped her coffee, enjoying the show.

"Your problem, you see, Marshall," Christopher continued, "is that you assumed everyone is like you. Motivated by greed and money and power. You assumed your ex would hit up her wealthy uncle for the money to pay us. You assumed Doug would do as he was told because you paid him. You assumed we'd do what you expected because there was money involved." Christopher finally shifted his gaze to Amato. "And you were wrong."

Amato slammed his hand on the table. This made the writer at the nearby table look up from his laptop, his eyes wide. Nina started to come around the counter, but Myra met her gaze and gave a small headshake. Nina remained out from behind the counter, but she stayed by Boo, watching the situation.

"You're the idiot," Amato said, his voice low and guttural. "And now that I have proof my ex was trying to steal from me, I'll have her and you all thrown in jail. I'll let her suffer there for a while before I have her killed, too. And her fucking uncle won't be able to do anything about it. I have proof." He raised the bag.

Myra blinked at him. "Of what, exactly?"

He glared at her. "Theft. That my ex-wife hired thieves to take my property. Doug recorded your entire conversation. I heard it."

"The property that is still in your home?" Myra said. "Or the property that, even as we speak, her uncle is retrieving after the court order that returns the heirloom to its rightful owner?"

Amato glared at Doug. "Did you fall for a fake? What the hell is going on? I thought you were a fixer? What the fuck?" He dug into the bag and pulled out the wooden box, flipping open the lid to investigate the silver chalices.

They were lovely pieces, engraved with swirling lines that looked like climbing ivy dotted with bundles of grapes. Each base was a solid circle, the stems narrow, the cups shaped to hold a significant amount of wine.

The little flaw in the design, the original artist's signature, appeared in one of the bundles of grapes near the base of the chalice, one single grape compressed into a quarter moon-shape instead of being a full circle. The flaw was in slightly different places on each cup, and very subtle in the silver etchings. But there if you knew what to look for.

Amato did not know what to look for.

Which was a shame. Since if he did know what to look for, he'd know he was holding the real chalices. And if he actually knew the history of the heirloom he'd stolen from his ex-wife, he'd understand why he shouldn't have opened the box and taken out the chalices. He certainly wouldn't have been studying them with his nose right against the silver. Definitely wouldn't have let his bare skin come into contact for that long with something made with magic.

If he'd ever had any idea what he'd actually had in his possession, he'd have realized he'd just poisoned himself by holding the real chalices.

Live and learn. Or in this case, he wouldn't live for much longer.

Doug was still staring at Christopher. "They're bluffing," he said to Amato. "That's the real heirloom." Doug half smiled, a strangely spooky expression. "Your ex will be getting a visit from the police within the hour."

"And my money?" Amato said.

"Should be clawed back and in your account in the next fifteen minutes."

Myra resisted laughing. Yeah, that wasn't happening. That money was long gone from the original account it had been wired to. But there was a lot of lying going on at that table. So she kept her amusement to herself.

"The video of the thieves?" Amato said with a snarl. "The recording you just made?"

"Already with the police," Doug assured.

"What happens when you die?" Myra asked casually. "All your stuff? Who gets it?"

"What the fuck are you talking about?" Amato said, trying to look smug but also flicking a worried glance at Doug.

"His ex-wife is still in the will to inherit everything,"

Christopher answered Myra's question—she already knew the answer, but she was enjoying watching Amato's confusion. "Prenup says he can't change the will. Her uncle ensured that part. Which means there's no way for him to avoid Una getting it all if he dies before her. So she needs to die before he does."

"Lot of smart talk for people about to go down for grand larceny. This heirloom is worth a fortune."

"You have no idea," Myra murmured.

"You should leave now," Doug said, his attention still on Christopher. "You don't want to be here with that when the police arrive."

"What if they get away?"

"They won't," Doug said. "You hired a fixer. Trust that I will fix things."

Amato smirked at them, closed the chalices back into the box and stuffed the whole thing back into the backpack. He slipped his sunglasses back on his face and stalked out of the coffee shop. Nina had the door open for him, giving him a falsely friendly nod as he walked out.

Having not actually touched anything inside the café.

Still, Nina came over with a clothe and some cleaner and cleaned the table and chair where Amato had been sitting. "He didn't set the chalice on the table, right?" she asked Myra.

"He did not," Myra assured. "And he didn't touch anything after he'd handled it."

Nina nodded, her attention on the table. "Never thought to see something like that in here."

Chalices of Destiny were very rare. Most people didn't survive long after coming into their possession. Unless they knew what they were doing.

Nina waved a hand over the table after she'd cleaned it with ordinary cleaners. A little blue glow covered the table, the chair, before fading away. Then she nodded. "There we go. All clean." She smiled at them. "Do you need more drinks? Anything to eat?"

"I would love another coffee, please," Myra said.

Christopher and Doug just shook their heads. They were *still* staring at each other.

Nina raised her brows at Myra. Myra shrugged. Men. What could you do?

Nina returned to the counter to make Myra's coffee and Myra watched the two men's staring contest quietly for a while.

When she was certain Amato was gone and not coming back, she said, "Una's uncle is a scary man."

Doug finally looked away from Christopher to smile at her. "He didn't take kindly to the way his niece was treated."

"Why didn't he just have you kill Amato outright?" Myra asked. "Why all this?" She waved her hand at the elaborate ruse they'd just perpetrated to get Amato to kill himself by handling magically poisoned chalices.

"He thought the punishment fit the crime," Doug said. "Una was always too…timid to fight back. Even when Amato was abusing her, she rarely discussed leaving. Probably why it blinded-sided Amato when she did finally leave. She knew what the chalices were, though, and was afraid Amato would figure it out and use them to harm people. Wanted them back to keep them safe. Amato never realized she was a sorceress. Probably for the best."

"Absolutely." Myra nodded. She didn't always have the best of experiences with sorcerers but in this case, she'd been happy to help play out the elaborate ruse. Una wasn't the kind of sorceress who used her skills for...well, much of anything. Like Myra, she'd inherited her powers from a relative, in Una's case, her grandmother. And unlike Myra, she'd decided to forgo following in her grandmother's footsteps.

Which was why Amato hadn't known what she was.

Una's uncle, however, had pursued the sorcerer path, like his mother, and that made him a powerful enemy for Amato. Amato had no idea what he was getting into, first marrying Una and then treating her so poorly. Hiring Doug only proved how ruthless and vindictive Una's uncle was.

The only reason Christopher had agreed to involve their team in this was because of Una herself. That old damsel in distress soft spot. If it had just been the uncle, they probably would have avoided the whole mess.

"So we're done here, then," Christopher said. "We have our money. You've succeeded in killing your target without him even knowing he's dead. I assume after she inherits everything, Una will find a safe spot to lock away those chalices."

There was a soft warning in Christopher's voice. Not so much a threat as an encouragement to do as he suggested.

"She will. Doesn't want them falling into the wrong hands." Doug shrugged. "Not even her uncle's."

Give her uncle was vicious enough to set up this level of revenge, yeah, probably best for him not to have a set of Destiny Chalices at his disposal.

Doug considered Myra for a moment and said, "You lied well. I wasn't expecting that. Almost believed you."

She grinned, but she didn't otherwise comment.

Doug let his many questions—questions she could see he wanted to ask—go and said instead, "My client would like to add a…tip to the money you got from Amato. That'll be in your account…" He looked at his cellphone screen. "Ah. Should be there now." He looked up, smiling. "I assume it's already being moved as well."

Christopher smiled tightly but didn't confirm.

Doug tipped his head. "Been a pleasure. Hopefully, we never meet again."

They watched him leave the café, watched until he'd disappeared into the crowded pedestrian traffic passing by the front windows.

"That was interesting," she said. "Kinda fun and scary at the same time." She turned in her chair to more fully face Christopher and caught the writer at the next table watching them. She raised her brows at him. "We better not end up in a book."

He quickly looked back down at his laptop, but Myra got the feeling some of this was definitely going into a novel. She couldn't really blame him. It had been pretty captivating stuff.

"I think we should avoid Una's uncle," she said to Christopher. "And Doug. I could do without working with Doug again."

"Or have him working against us."

"That." Myra finished her coffee. Then bumped her shoulder against Christopher's arm. "Told you this place was perfect for this. Even got the table and chairs magically sterilized."

"You were right."

"Wait, say that again." She tilted her head to one side, putting her ear closer to him. "Repeat that please."

His deep chuckle made her stomach tighten and a thick, delicious warmth spread through her.

"Let's go check on the others, and all that money. Then… pizza? My treat."

"So long as it's thin crust, I'm in."

They bickered about the pros and cons of thick crust on the way out, but Myra stopped long enough to thank Nina. "Sorry about bringing trouble into the café," she said. "But I knew we'd be safe doing…that here."

"Fair enough. No one got hurt. You bought a lot of coffee. And I just checked my bank account and there's a sizable…tip that's been added. So, I guess I should say, thank you."

Myra gave Boo a little scritch on the head, and then headed out with Christopher. On the sidewalk, she said, "You arranged the tip for Nina?"

"Figured it was the least we could do. Wasn't entirely sure how that would turn out."

"You are a big old softy," she said and jumped up into his arms.

He caught her without missing a beat. "I could be persuaded to be…harder later."

The not-so-subtle innuendo made her entire body warm. Christopher had a way of doing that to her. And she absolutely loved it.

Loved even more when his dragon wings erupted from his back and he launched into the sky, flying them back to their people, their rewards, and later, to their own private celebration. The perfect way to end a good con.

JAMAR AT THE CAFÉ

JAMAR

Jamar hadn't played his guitar in weeks. Maybe months. He couldn't seem to bring himself to pick it up. There was something about strumming the strings, letting the low vibrations filter through his arms and bones, the hum of the music…

He missed that feel, those sounds, and yet he couldn't seem to get back to it.

Always one thing or another. Some crisis. His dad getting kicked out of a club he'd joined last fall for arguing with the club president—it was a card playing club, but the argument had been over politics and his activist father had *not* backed down. Jamar was proud of his dad, but now his dad was restless and bored and kept pulling Jamar into activities that had nothing to do with Jamar's music.

His mother had been taking care of her aging mother for the last few months, which had taken a toll, so Jamar kept stopping in at the house to take up some of the slack for his mom. And occasionally take a shift with his grandmother to give his mom a break.

The sessions he'd had booked at a local studio, playing backup guitar for various singers coming through, had all been cancelled because the studio had some legal trouble with its landlord and had to shut down for a few months. That had left Jamar a little low on cash. He worked at a local music store and taught guitar lessons on the side, which helped cover the bills, but his work at the studio was what he wanted to do.

He had no interest in fame or playing in a band. But he did want to make a living with music.

It was just, at the moment, that had gotten a little hard. And life was a little more complicated.

Which made losing himself in the music feel impossible.

He only realized it had been months since he'd played when his mother asked how his music was going and he hadn't been able to tell her anything.

That realization was what drove him to the café with his guitar case in hand. One of his guitars. The acoustic one. He used electric guitars in the studio sessions, and alternated between acoustics and electric for the lessons—depending on the student. But this was his muck about guitar. The one he took to random parks and restaurants and coffee shops, and even once or twice to the library, to play. Just for fun.

The café was relatively new, at least to him. A place that had only opened a few weeks ago. But it had a nice vibe. He'd gone in after being at the studio to collect some of his gear until they reopened and instantly liked the place. The feel of it was just…comfortable. The kind of place you could sit and sip coffee and eat muffins and enjoy your own company for hours and no one bothered you.

The place was attached to a nice independent bookstore, the two businesses flowing between each other through a wide opening in one wall. The café part itself had been a lot of wooden chairs and tall tables when he'd first come in, but since, the owner had rearranged some things and set out more couches and cushioned chairs and low tables like coffee tables and side tables. The center of the seating area was still more standard circular tables and chairs, but the edges were all comfortable seating arrangements like someone's living room.

The owner's name was Nina and she was very nice. A little rushed off her feet because the coffee shop did good business. But the last time Jamar had been in here, she'd had an assistant helping her. And there was a giant Maine coon cat that called a stool near the register his home. His name was Boo. He was huge, and pale gray, with pale blue eyes, all of which made his name fit really well.

Jamar had a take 'em or leave 'em attitude toward pets. But he did like cats. He wouldn't consider owning one. But he liked the way they sometimes purred. His brother had a cat which he didn't mind at all. His sister's dogs were too chaotic. Sweet, but chaos on legs. Too much constant energy for Jamar.

During his two previous visits to the café, Jamar hadn't bothered bringing his guitar, but this time, he decided it might be a good idea. A way to get back to playing that wasn't pressured, like a studio gig. He was starting to feel like if he didn't pick the guitar up again, he might never want to, and that feeling was horrible. But at home, or at work, actually playing had felt…impossible.

Whatever the block was, he was hoping the café would help him climb over it.

And if it didn't, well, at least the coffee was good.

He sat at a table against the wall near the register, not far from Boo and his stool. Nina and her assistant Akira were busy that day—a weekend—and constantly moving behind the counter or out into the seating area to deliver drinks. He got his oat milk coffee at the counter and carried it himself to his table. He liked this spot. He could see a lot of the sitting area and the front door to the café, and look across into the bookstore, but he also felt sort of shielded from the rest of the room. Tucked into a corner where no one paid him any attention.

He was starting to recognize a few people here. The older woman, sitting in the center of the dining area, engrossed in a book—he couldn't see the title, but last time he'd been nosy enough to check, she seemed to be reading erotica. The middle-aged white man sitting near the back, pounding away on his laptop. There was also another white man, who looked a bit like a lawyer, sitting at the front window of the café. That man spent a lot of time glancing at Nina, and Nina spent a lot of time glancing back at him. It was a love song waiting to happen, and made Jamar grin. If he could get back to playing his guitar, maybe he'd write that song. He wasn't much of a song writer. In his deepest soul, he was a studio musician. But he dabbled.

Once settled, he sipped his drink, with just the right amount of oat milk to sharp black coffee, trying to work himself up to taking out his guitar. Just a few notes. Maybe run some chord progressions. Just a few minutes of play to break the cycle. He was certain once he set the old guitar on his lap, wrapped his long fingers around the neck, settled the pick between his right fingers, he'd be able to play without trouble. That was what he did after all, right? He played guitar.

Instead of opening his case, though, he pulled out his phone and ear buds and started listening to one of the new bands a friend at the music shop had told him about. They were playing a gig in a week, and his friend thought they might be a group Jamar would love. They only had one album out so far, and were an indie group without a big label. Jamar liked that part. He'd seen the damage some of those big labels could do to unique bands. Some groups were better off staying small and independent. But, of course, that wasn't his place to say for other people. Not everyone wanted the music just for the sake of the music. More people wanted to be rich from their music than Jamar would have suspected before getting involved in the industry.

But according to Doug, this group was one of the ones who just wanted to improve their craft and entertain their audiences. Eclectic and innovative. The kind of musical range Jamar loved.

He told himself this was research. That part of his job

was listening to new bands, absorbing music all the time, studying innovative new guitarists. And the woman leading this band was one of the most innovative guitarists Jamar had heard in a long time, too.

But his still firmly-closed guitar case leaning against the wall next to his cushioned seat was a constant reminder that he was here to attempt playing again, without any pressure, and he was failing in that effort.

He glanced over at the cat sitting on his stool and realized Boo was staring at him. Guess he did have an audience after all. When Boo didn't do anything more than just sit there staring, Jamar started to get uncomfortable. Why the hell was that cat staring at him?

Maybe if he focused on something else.

He glanced out the window, looked around the café, turned his attention to his half empty coffee mug. Maybe he should get some more coffee. Didn't want to take up a seat when he wasn't paying for the place.

But when he looked toward the register, Boo was still staring at him and getting up to stand next to the cat felt like a good way of getting swiped by sharpened claws. Not sure why he was worried about that. Boo wasn't hissing at him. Wasn't glaring—any more than a cat's natural stare kinda felt like a glare. The cat was just…watching him.

Desperate to do something, anything to distract himself from that stare, he actually set his mug down and reached for the guitar case. Flicking open the latches, pulling the acoustic out of the soft interior. The feel of the wooden neck settling into his hand, the weight of the base in his lap, slipping the pick out of the strings out of habit. Familiar. Like settling into his own body.

He'd had a guitar in his arms since the age of nine and it was such a familiar position now, he wondered that he'd been able to go so long without picking one up.

After a moment, the music still playing in his ears settled into his fingertips. He let his fingers dance over the strings without actually strumming, his eyes half closed as he listened to the excellent guitarist power through a complex solo that ran up and down the neck. Could he play something under that, a counter to steady it and make it stand out more?

He moved his fingers over the strings again, and this time thrummed gently with the pick, not trying to even make noise, but feeling the music that *would* come out if he put in the effort. The sound was there, right there, and it made him smile.

Another sound rose up next to him. A sound that was not guitar. He looked to the seat armrest where Boo had hopped up, balancing his huge body as only a cat could. Staring at the guitar now. When Jamar looked at him, Boo looked up and met his gaze, then looked back at the guitar.

And purred.

The purr sounded weirdly in tune with the music playing in Jamar's ears. He frowned a little as he stared at Boo, but also started playing. Louder this time, just enough he could hear the notes he produced alongside the music in his ears and the sound of Boo's purr. The combination was odd, and interesting. And lyrical.

He smiled. "You wanna jam?" he asked Boo.

Boo wrapped his fluffy tail around his legs, still perched on the armrest like it wasn't much too small for him, and the purr turned up to eleven. Jamar chuckled, and raced along the chords to keep up with the guitarist he was listening to, matching Boo's tone and rhythm. The whole thing was a little chaotic but also fun. Weird and yet beautiful. A race around a song they were making up as they went. Not quite the one he was listening to. A sort of rock and roll jazz progression that probably didn't sound as interesting to anyone in the café as it sounded to him.

Except maybe Boo.

Because Boo just kept purring along with him. And if Jamar was the fanciful type, he'd swear that cat was grinning as he purred.

Jamar let the music he was playing wind down in time with the music in his ears, an impactful note from the band's lead singer resonating for a hanging moment before the song ended. He paused for a long time, staring at Boo, who had stopped purring in perfect time to the end of the music. Then he smiled. And Boo smiled back—he was sure of it, even if most of the smile seemed to be in the cat's eyes.

Jamar set his guitar aside, placing it gently in the guitar case at his feet and snapping the lid closed. Then he straightened, picked up his mostly cool coffee and sipped it. Boo's eyes narrowed slightly.

"Fine," Jamar said. "I'll get another cup."

Boo gave another one of those smiles that came mostly from his eyes and curled up on the chair armrest, seemingly unconcerned that his body was five times too big for that perch.

Jamar went and got another oat milk coffee, then sat next to Boo and tapped his foot while he listened to more of the new band's album. Occasionally, Boo purred along.

For the first time in a while, Jamar felt more like himself, like the guitar and his music weren't so far out of reach.

When he finally had to leave to get to work, he looked at Boo. "Up for another session tomorrow?"

Boo licked his paw and Jamar would swear the cat nodded at him.

He laughed. "Okay. Guess I'll see you then."

He ambled out, looking forward to tomorrow's jam session with a café cat named Boo.

NINA AND BOO AND RHYS WITHERBY TOO

NINA AND BOO AND RHYS

Nina hurried back and forth between the register and the espresso machine, making coffees and chatting with customers and generally enjoying the buzz of a busy Saturday. Her usual assistant for Saturdays, Akira, was off for the day thanks to an eye doctor's appointment, so it was just Nina working the counter. But she didn't mind.

Because he was here. Sitting at his usual table at the front of the café, near one of the windows. Though in the last month, his usual table had become a low, rectangular coffee table surrounded by deep cushioned seats that were easy to lounge in.

She'd just recently decided the café wasn't comfy enough and had started moving in couches and cushioned chairs, leaving a few of the ordinary tables and chairs in the center of the seating area, but arranging clusters and nooks around the edges where people could be more comfortable lingering with their drinks. Learning how to run the café and ensure it was a nice place to visit was taking her some time. But she really loved the place and how it was evolving. She loved the different customers that came in and out from the attached bookstore. The regulars that had established their "place" in the coffeeshop.

There was Frank in one of the older table and chairs near the back of the café, pounding away at his laptop, his mug of coffee refreshed at his elbow, the plate where she'd left him a couple of croissants empty.

There was Agnes with her mug of tea steaming in front of her as she read yet another erotica book, this one a book of Best Of stories for the year. She sat at one of the older tables and chairs in the very center of the café, a position which gave her a good view of the front door, the bookstore entrance, and the counter. That had become Agnes' place.

Jamar, the musician who sometimes played his guitar, had taken one of the coffee table and cushioned chairs near the counter. Boo really liked Jamar, so the giant Maine coon often left his perch on a too-small stool next to the register and jumped up on the chair arm next to Jamar for a jam session. Sometimes they just ignored each other. They got along like a house on fire.

Amir, a student at the local university, used one of the older tables in the middle of the café to study and pound coffees. They always went out through the bookstore instead of the café's main entrance, and the bookstore owner said they always bought a book on their way out. Either a science fiction novel or a historical romance.

There was Diana, who Nina was half convinced was an actual goddess—*the* Diana—but she hadn't admitted that yet. Diana mostly drank cappuccinos and loved the chocolate muffins, and kept to the wall right beside the bookstore entrance, reading fashion and hunting magazines, and occasionally a doorstop-sized fantasy novel. She'd happily adjusted to the new couches and cushioned chairs too, though she preferred the larger side tables to the low coffee tables for her drinks.

And then there was…him.

Rhys Witherby. He claimed to be a lawyer who worked in the area. She hadn't argued with him about that. She was claiming to be a café owner who was the age she looked— somewhere in her thirties—rather than the much older witch with the familiar who looked like a Maine coon cat.

Rhys liked croissants and milky lattes on his days off. Black coffee with sugar on his work days. He liked to sit near the front window. He had an excellent smile. Smelled delicious, sort of woodsy pine. And had been coming in and out of the café since it first opened.

He also occasionally helped her if things went pear-shaped or something weird happened in the café. And he seemed unfazed by the weirder situations that tended toward things like, oh, real goddesses, and the occasional goblin, and that woman who had a dragon companion, and the one who was a Protector—though technically Nina wasn't supposed to know Protectors existed. She wasn't sure Rhys new what that woman was, but he'd been at the ready to help if needed.

And he'd never asked questions or seemed surprised by any of the strange stuff. The things that one might consider… well, fictional. Given they were attached to a bookstore and a lot of people considered books magic, Nina—especially because she was a witch—liked that idea and had seen enough evidence of it spilling over into the café that she had started to believe all bookstores were magic. But her life was, even without the bookstore, filled with magic. And a nagging familiar. And the occasional bit of magical intervention.

Rhys claimed to be an ordinary lawyer. Ordinary lawyers didn't take paranormal and supernatural events with a casual shrug.

Her curiosity about him wasn't helped by the fact that she'd been melting over his smiles since they met.

For months now, they'd been dancing around each other, chatting and smiling and not revealing too much but just enough to always have something to talk about. He sat in his usual place. Drank his coffees, ate his pastries, and when he was done, stopped at the counter to say goodbye and let her know when he'd be back.

But…that was it.

He hadn't asked her out. Asked for a phone number. Asked if she got a day off work—she did thanks to Akira but not all that often. He'd asked what she liked to eat besides pastries and coffee but then never followed that up with an invitation to dinner.

Nina wasn't usually the kind of woman who waited

around for a crush to ask her out if he was showing interest. If there was mutual attraction, and he seemed shy about broaching the topic of spending more time together, she brought it up. She wasn't particularly shy after all these years. But with him…

She adjusted her apron, hurried to get her current customer her to-go cup of coffee with almond milk, and tired not to let the giddiness in her stomach affect her coffee.

Having a crush like this was both exhilarating and ridiculous. Made her excited to come to work every day. And also left her feeling like an idiot who really should be too old for this kind of thing.

That afternoon, with Rhys in his usual seat but no Akira to cover all the extra work, Nina spent most of her time running around serving customers with barely enough room to breathe. She managed to bus tables and get some of the dishes washed in the few lulls, but most of the day was hectic. She didn't mind. Being busy was a lot better than being bored. She'd take busy every time.

Boo remained at his perch on the stool next to the register, pretending to be an ordinary pale gray cat with pale blue eyes whose name suited his general fluffy ghost look. He snoozed, or appeared to, and people watched his days away at the café. And since Jamar wasn't in at the moment, Boo remained nearby. He didn't talk to her during the day— too many of the customers were just ordinary people and wouldn't understand a talking cat—so his guise as an ordinary cat worked.

Nina was pretty sure Rhys, and probably Agnes, knew what Boo was. She was pretty sure Diana knew too, but Diana and Boo ignored each other so thoroughly it was hard to tell. Agnes at least occasionally gave Boo a scritch when she ordered her tea. And Boo purred for Agnes.

Boo purred for Rhys, too, but Nina suspected that was more because Nina had a crush on him and Boo liked to stir the pot. So to speak.

On this particularly busy day, Rhys seemed to linger longer in his seat by the window, nursing his milky coffee, though his croissant was long gone. He kept his gaze out the window, his expression distant.

Her curiosity almost had her going over to ask if he wanted to talk about whatever seemed to be bothering him. But she was too busy for that kind of break, her attention would be divided. And if he did want to talk, she wanted to give him her full attention.

Still, she watched him from the corner of her eye. He showed no signs of leaving, even after his coffee was done. Just sat and stared out the window.

At three in the afternoon, a lull in new customers gave her a chance to break away from the espresso machine. The bookstore seemed busy, a lot of people wandering the stacks, but no new café patrons came through either the front door or the open wall between bookstore and café.

Boo looked up at her from his perch on his stool, his pale blue eyes narrowed. His fluffy pale gray fur spiked along his spine, which meant something wasn't quite right. They'd been together long enough they'd found ways to communicate even without words.

Boo was ensuring she knew something was wrong.

When she cut her gaze to Rhys, Boo licked his paw.

So. Whatever the problem was, it did have to do with Rhys. And now Nina really wanted to know what was going on.

She skirted around the counter, collected a few empty mugs and left them in the plastic wash bin on a stand next to the counter—some customers returned their plates and mugs to the bin, others expected her to bus the tables. She did, and didn't really mind, but her favorite customers were the ones who tidied up after themselves. She liked people who took the people around them into consideration.

Once she had the few tables that needed it cleared, she wiped her hands off on her apron and slowly approached Rhys.

He looked up when she was within talking distance, and despite his earlier pensive expression, he smiled at her. "Nina," he greeted. Then he blinked and looked around. "You actually got a break in the traffic, huh?"

"Yeah. Not sure how long it will last." She smiled, try to force a lightness into her voice, but worry made the tone sound wrong to her ears. "You want another coffee? Or maybe one of the new fruit tarts? I have two left."

"Thanks. No. I'm good." He glanced down at the table, a furrow between his brows. "I should… I should probably go."

"Oh. Okay. Well. Sure. Yeah. Saturday and everything. Probably have a lot to do."

She started to clear his coffee mug, but he briefly touched her wrist, stilling her mid-motion. He didn't grab her arm or touch her beyond that brief contact. When he looked up at her, he was frowning.

"Do you have a minute to…" He glanced out the window, then gave a short nod and said, "I need to talk to you for a minute if you have time."

"Sure." She dropped into the cushioned seat opposite him. She'd have been a bit giddy about getting a chance to talk to him in something more than a fleeting way—and wasn't that embarrassing for someone her age—but he looked so serious, her worry overwhelmed any delight.

"I'm sorry," he started.

"For?"

"I think I might have…" He glanced out the window again. "I shouldn't have come in so often. I think I've brought the wrong kind of attention to your café."

She narrowed her eyes and then followed his gaze out the window. She didn't see anything at first, just busy sidewalks and the open clothing boutique across the street. The Italian restaurant. The drugstore.

But something tickled an instinct. Something felt…off.

Under her breath, she murmured a spell and passed her hand over her eyes.

And there. Now she saw him. Standing in the shadows across the road, back against the brick wall between the boutique and the restaurant. He was tall, and slim. Dressed in a dark gray suit, but no coat though it was a cool enough day. People walked by him on the sidewalk without turning to look. One person seemed to almost bump off him without seeing him. That person frowned and shivered as they moved down the street.

"Who is he?" she asked.

Rhys glanced at her. "You can see him?"

"Now. Who is he?"

Rhys nodded. "His name is Virgil."

"Like the Roman poet?"

This earned her a fleeting smile. "Like the Roman poet." His expression turned serious again. "He's…not a poet."

"I got that impression. What is he?"

"A vampire." Rhys met her gaze. He'd said that starkly and without prevaricating. Almost challenging. As if he excepted her to balk, or laugh, or dismiss the comment.

If that's what he was waiting for, he'd be waiting for some time.

She did frown, though, and ask, "Who can disguise his presence in the middle of the day?"

That wasn't a typical vampire skill. At least not one she'd encountered before. To be fair, she avoided vampires as much as possible. Their machinations and politics gave her a headache. She preferred staying under the radar. But after eight decades, she'd had no choice but to learn something about vampires.

Rhys gave her a considering look. Then nodded to himself before saying, "He's unusual for his kind. He was a wizard before being turned. His magic went with him into his new undead life." Rhys sighed. "And made him even more dangerous than the usual vampire."

"Oh good," she said, with no little sarcasm.

Rhys chuckled, though there was an edge to it. "I wasn't excepting you to…"

"Accept that there are vampires?"

"Admit that you knew about them so easily," he finished. "You're very good at…at being human. And ordinary."

"Thanks?"

He smiled. "It was supposed to be a compliment. Sorry. Having Virgil here has thrown me off my game."

"So you do have game, then?"

This earned her a more natural sounding chuckle. She liked that sound.

Shame they had to go back to worrying about the vampire.

"Let's just say I've seen some things and vampires are not the most unusual of those things."

His gaze skimmed over the people sitting around the café. Briefly, he paused at Agnes. And then Diana. His attention lingered on Boo, too. Then he met her gaze and nodded.

She didn't confirm or deny any of the implications of those looks. Though if he knew about vampires, he likely knew about witches and familiars. Even she wasn't sure what Agnes was. But she wondered if he'd realized Diana was likely a goddess.

"What's the vampire doing here?" she asked, returning to the subject at hand. "And why is he hovering around across the street?"

"Why he's across the street is the easier question to answer," Rhys said. "It's because he likes letting me know he knows where I am. He won't come in here. At least not yet. But…since this is a business and therefore open, he can come in without an invitation."

She nodded. "The implied invitation that comes with being open to the public."

Vampires couldn't enter private homes without an invitation—and were devilish good at getting that invitation if a hapless human wasn't careful—but businesses didn't have the same universal protection. There was an *implied* invitation once an establishment opened its doors for business. Her café and the bookstore next door were both wide open to vampires.

And normally, she wouldn't be too worried about that. They were only open during the day, with only a few hours of evening darkness in the winter. Vampires could come out during the day. No ash and instant death just because sunshine. But they were weaker in the sun. None of the things that made them extremely dangerous were in their skill set during the day. They might still be a touch stronger than the average human, but not by much. They moved at normal human speeds. They couldn't use mesmerism—their actual greatest skill above speed and strength. Even their ability to pierce the skin with their teeth and suck blood was extra hard during the day.

So daylight business hours meant vampires weren't a major threat—this was one of the main reasons a lot of businesses, and in fact a large part of human life, ran during the day rather than overnight. Scary things were less scary in all that sunlight. And easier to see coming.

But up to this point in her admittedly new business, Nina hadn't seen a vampire inside the bookstore or the café.

Especially not a vampire who was also a magic wielding former wizard.

That was a new combination for her. The magic usually didn't survive the death and rising.

"So he's here because of you," she said. "And he's particularly dangerous because of his magic. Does the magic work during the day?" Magic didn't usually have time-of-day restrictions, but this was magic in a vampire, magic that had returned to the vampire when he rose from the dead. The rules might have changed.

"It does, I'm sorry to say. But…not like it did when he was a human."

"Stronger or weaker during the day?"

"The magic? Actually stronger than it is at night."

"Well that's inconvenient."

Rhys chuckled, though he sounded strained again. "Very. It means he doesn't have the usual…weak time that a vampire would. It's just he has different skills to worry about, depending on the time of day and amount of sunlight he's standing in."

Because of daylight weakness, most vampires preferred to spend days deep underground, in places were no sunlight reached them. They didn't grow weak if they weren't out in the sun. And, especially with Masters trying to maintain a hive, most vampires *hated* showing weakness. That was the real reason they mostly avoided daylight and the sun. Not because they couldn't be out in it, but because they didn't *want* to be out in it and show their weakness.

Apparently, Virgil did not have the same problem.

She considered Rhys in silence for another few moments. When he didn't continue with his explanations, she said, "Are you avoiding telling me why he's taunting you? Or is that something you *can't* tell me? Which is okay. You don't have to. Really, it's none of my business."

She wanted it to be her business, of course. Finding out that Rhys was, shall we say, more *aware* of the supernatural side of life was a relief to be honest. She'd suspected. But now she knew for sure. Their cards were on the table now. At least, a couple of them. She still hadn't admitted out loud what she was, and he hadn't admitted out loud how he knew about the hidden worlds. But at least they both now knew they knew…something.

Since it had taken her ages just to screw up the brain cells to remember to ask his name, she could give him all the time he wanted before revealing his secrets. If he ever did. Which wasn't a guarantee. Even if she was very curious.

"It's not that I can't tell you," Rhys said, his gaze moving back across the street.

Nina followed the look. The vampire was still hovering in the shadows. When Nina looked at him, he smiled and tipped his oversized black hat at her. She blinked. Not because he'd spotted her looking at him but because he hadn't had a hat on just a moment ago and she hadn't seen him holding one.

"It's that I'm afraid if I do tell you," Rhys continued,

"I'm worried you'll ask me not to come back." He shrugged. "I like it here. I'd like to keep coming back."

The fact that he was worried she'd banish him from her café sounded ominous. "If you can tell me what you're trying not to say, it would help alleviate my suspicions and probably I wouldn't kick you out then." Maybe. Depended on what he had to say.

But she would hate to learn he wasn't the man she'd been hoping he was. She'd miss his smile.

Rhys sighed and leaned back in his cushioned chair, looking resigned. He met her gaze, his mouth flat, as he said, "Virgil is my brother. And, when I'm not doing my job as a lawyer… I'm a vampire hunter."

"I see."

"But that's not the worst of it."

"It's not?"

"I'm also…a wizard."

***

Well. That was a lot to take in one admission. Nina leaned back in her own cushioned seat and stared at Rhys Witherby. As if seeing him for the first time. The man she'd been crushing on for a while now was still there. But there was a whole new aspect to him, a whole new facet that changed her impression of him.

She was surprised to realize this new facet didn't detract from her impression. In fact, she found herself even more fascinated by him. And that was odd enough she had to take a moment to process it all.

Boo jumped down from his perch on his stool by the register and wandered over to them as they stared at each other. He jumped up onto the cushioned chair next to her, circled once, and settled half on her lap, half in the oversized chair next to her. His reassuring purr soothed her as she stroked her hand down his soft pale gray fur.

As they both stared at Rhys.

Rhys, for his part, didn't flinch from those stares. He met her gaze, awaiting her judgment, not hiding or trying to rush her.

She appreciated that.

The problem with Rhys being a wizard was that witches and wizards were notoriously ill suited to keep company with each other. It happened. There were even committed romantic relationships that involved wizards and witches. But it was…rare.

Witches and wizards weren't gender designations for the same kind of magic. You could have male witches and female wizards and nonbinary or transgendered or genderfluid practitioners of either type of magic. The labels Wizard and Witch described the type of magic wielded, not the person doing the wielding.

And those different uses of magic sometimes clashed. Wizards were more brute force and power. Witches leaned more toward spells and potions. Where witches could utilize illusion spells and curses, wizards were more likely to create objects infused with magic—cursed or not—and toss around bolts of energy.

Witch magic often took time, from a few seconds to days or months depending on what was brewing. Wizard magic tended to happen fast, but also burned out quickly.

And, historically speaking, melding those two magics into a single coherent life between people could be complicated.

But she was getting ahead of herself. So far, she had a crush and some exchanged smiles with Rhys. There hadn't even been an exchange of phone numbers. Worrying about the fact that he was a wizard was definitely premature.

Though, the fact that Boo had come to sit in her lap during this conversation spoke volumes.

"So. Virgil Witherby? Interesting name for a vampire."

"Our father was into Roman history. Mother liked all things Welsh. They each got their choice for one son."

"Just the two of you? No other siblings?"

"No other siblings."

"I have a lot of questions."

"I thought you might."

"I'm not going to ask them all right now."

His jaw worked with some suppressed emotion she couldn't read. "But you'll ask later?"

"If you're willing to answer, I'm curious enough I probably will."

"That means…you'll let me come back to the café?"

"I have no reason to ban you from the place." Yet. But she was pretty sure, based on past behavior, he wouldn't give her a reason. At least, she hoped he wouldn't. "For now, I would like to know why your brother, the vampire wizard, is taunting you, the vampire hunter wizard."

"And lawyer."

"Can't forget that part."

"Most offensive part according to any number of people I've talked to," he said.

She tried not to chuckle and failed. "Ah, lawyers aren't so bad."

"How about vampire hunters and wizards?"

"Depends on who they are. You still haven't answered my question."

"I'm stalling. He's out there taunting me because…" Rhys sighed. "Because I… I like it here."

"Is he a threat to anyone in my café? Or in the bookstore?" The owner of the bookstore was just an ordinary human woman, lovely as she was, so Nina felt a responsibility for looking after that half of the business too.

"Not today."

"In the future?"

"Depends."

"This is like pulling teeth, Rhys. Would you prefer not to tell me?"

"Yes, but mostly because I don't want you thinking less of me."

"I don't. I'm actually quite fond of you. If you're going to tell me anything, please do. All in one go. Then we can go deal with your brother."

"Deal with him?"

"That'll depend on what you tell me." She did have a spell for keeping vampires away from her door. Even an open business door. But it was a general spell and would keep all vampires out, and frankly, some of them weren't all that bad. She'd hate to ban them from the café and bookstore just because. She hated the idea of banning any potential customers.

"Fond of me?"

"We'll come back to that topic. Your brother first."

He gave a nod, but something moved through his expression that made her stomach dance. Probably she should be too old for crushes and those little zings of excitement when her crush looked at her that way. She was not. But she probably should have been.

"It might seem…contrary to his nature," Rhys started, his voice quiet and deep, "but my brother doesn't like most vampires. He could never abide a hive structure. Even if he were the Master. He… He was turned against his will. On a hunt."

"He was a vampire hunter before? And a wizard? Like you?"

"He was. Is." He shook his head. "We worked together before. Sometimes we had to work alone, though. When he was turned… He went out without me because I was busy with work. An important case. I can't really talk about it. NDAs and client privilege, but it was important. So he left me to it and went hunting a particularly nasty vampire on his own. He shouldn't have tried it. He thought his magic would give him the edge. It usually did. But this was a

Master and an old, mean one at that. Not a clever one. But vicious."

Nina got that. She'd heard things. Even avoiding vampires, it was impossible not to hear things in her world.

"Anyway, the turning was a kind of punishment to us both. The Master thought he'd be able to control my brother after, get my brother to kill me." Rhys rubbed a hand over his face and then looked out the window again, in the direction of his brother. "We'd made a deal, a long time ago, to ensure neither was turned. But I didn't get to him in time to prevent… By the time I found him, the deed was done."

"I'm sorry," Nina murmured.

Rhys nodded absently, his gaze still across the street. "We discussed whether I should kill him or not. I didn't want to. He wanted me to. At first."

This time Nina didn't ask all the questions she had. She let Rhys finish in his own time.

"When we realized he'd kept his magic after the change, and that the Master who'd turned him couldn't control him, we…made a new plan." Rhys finally looked at her. "We still hunt vampires."

"Ah." She nodded. So. The wizard turned vampire used his new nature to help in the hunt. "Did you kill the Master?"

"We haven't yet. When he realized he couldn't control Virgil, he vanished. We haven't been able to find him."

"Shame." It would have been some kind of justice if they'd been able to kill him after all.

"Virgil is here because…" Rhys swallowed. "The last time I was distracted, it was work, and he suffered for it. I've been dutiful in my legal work since, but not to the exclusion of our work. The legal work comes second. That's my repayment to Virgil for failing him last time. Nothing comes between me and our hunts anymore."

She didn't comment. She wasn't sure that was a healthy response, but she also understood it at a deep level, so she wasn't going to pass judgments or give advice. Wasn't her place to do so anyway.

"He's here because he thinks something might be starting to come between me and our work again."

"A client?"

"You."

Nina blinked. "Oh."

That was…thrilling was probably the wrong emotion but there it was. Her stomach dancing, a smile trying to escape, a tingling of excitement racing over her skin. She probably shouldn't be so delighted to be a distraction to him, but it meant this crush of hers wasn't a one-way thing and that was delightful. Even if the timing was not the best.

"Virgil might be dangerous to you if he thinks you're getting in the way."

"Why dangerous?"

"He wasn't unaffected by the turning. He's not the man he was before. Some of my brother is still there. That's why we can continue to hunt together. But he's…angrier. More sly and vicious." Rhys huffed, a sound that held no humor when he said, "More bloodthirsty."

"I see." Nina glanced down at Boo. Boo looked up at her, his pale blue eyes steady as he blinked slowly. His pupils were narrowed in the bright sunlight coming in through the windows next to them, making his pale eyes even paler. He looked like the ghost he was named for. "Okay," she said after a moment.

"Okay…what?" Rhys asked, looking leery and uncertain.

"Let's go talk to your brother."

Boo came with her, walking at her side, as she stepped out onto the sidewalk. Before leaving the café, she asked Agnes to keep an eye on things, knowing the older woman wouldn't let anything untoward happen. And knowing, or at least being pretty sure, Agnes would understand this was not an ordinary human situation.

The day was cool and breezy, a sharp scent of approaching winter in the air. The fall had that quality of light she loved, fading but still bright. It was hard to explain but she could feel the seasons turning and the feel of autumn was her favorite.

She'd left on her apron, but because the café had been warm, she'd been wearing a short sleeve t-shirt with the café's logo on the front as she worked. The cold breeze made her skin tingle now.

Rhys followed her outside, moving to stand beside her. "Are you sure about this?"

"Certain." This was her place of business and she had no intention of letting a vampire disrupt things. Or threaten her.

Or his own brother for that matter. Rhys was welcome in her café for as long as he wanted to visit.

The rest…

Well, that wasn't any of his brother's business.

Virgil remained where he was in the shadows across the street, not moving for a long moment. But the smirk he'd been flashing her and Rhys while they sat inside the café had vanished. And she could just see the glitter of yellow in his eyes beneath the wide brim of his hat.

After a full minute of just staring at each other, Virgil finally tipped his hat at them, stepped away from the wall that had shadowed him, and moved across the street. He didn't bother checking for traffic—either pedestrian or car—and nothing and no one got in his way.

"Nice trick," she said. Not raising her voice. He was a vampire. He'd hear her. Even in the sunlight.

Virgil's smirk returned as he joined them on the sidewalk. "Rhys," he greeted. "How unexpected finding you here."

Nina rolled her eyes. She couldn't help it. "I like sarcasm as much as the next person," she said, "but can we manage without it for a few minutes. We have something to settle."

"Do we?" Virgil shifted his smirk to her, but the expression faded to something significantly more threatening. And the yellow in his eyes glittered.

She felt the push of his magic then. Not a hit of power, just a little brush of it, a flicker of raw magic to rub against her skin. It created a nails-on-chalkboard irritation that made the hairs on her arms rise. Boo let out a very quiet growling hiss.

Nina murmured a word, pressed a button on her apron, and shook her head as her protective shield came up. "Don't test me, wizard. This isn't my first rodeo."

"How old are you, witch?"

"Old enough to know that's a rude question."

This brought out a reluctant smile that still looked more like a smirk. "He's too easily distracted, but I can see why. In this case."

"I'm flattered?"

"No offense," Virgil said.

"Right."

"We have work to do." He dropped the pleasantries and the reluctant smile. "You interfere."

"I would never interfere in vampire hunters doing their job," she said. "Not very fond of vampires myself."

"Ouch?"

"No offense."

"Right," he said.

She held his gaze, a staring contest that normally would have been a very stupid move with a vampire. Even in the daylight, she could feel the pull of his thrall. He was very strong as a vampire if she could feel that at this time of day. That combined with his wizard's magic would make him a formidable enemy. She wasn't here to make enemies. But she wasn't going to be intimidated either.

And it was daylight after all. His mesmerism wasn't dominant enough to pull her under right now. Not through her shield. Not with Boo at her side.

Boo rubbed against her leg, giving her that magical

balance and boost that a witch got from their long-time familiar.

Virgil's steady gaze flicked to his brother after a moment, when it became clear he wouldn't be able to roll her under in the middle of the day. She wouldn't be able to play that game at night, though. His brush of magic had given her a very good sense of the flavor and strength of that part of his nature. And that was strong as well. Not a wizard she'd take lightly.

But then, she wasn't the sort of witch to be taken lightly either.

To his brother, he said, "I get it. But it's a distraction. And you promised me no more distraction."

"I promised no more work distractions. This isn't work."

"No." Virgil redirected his intense stare to Nina. "It's not."

"It's coffee," Nina said. "And pastries. You should try some. You might like them." Vampires could eat food if they really wanted to. Most just felt no need to consume solid food. And honestly, if they were going to, pastries wouldn't have been top of the list. But the croissants and muffins she served were really good.

"Don't be obtuse," Virgil said. "Or attempt to be funny. This is a life or death choice for him." Virgil looked at his brother. "And it is a choice. Life or death. Because when you get distracted, someone dies."

Before Nina could comment, Virgil turned and walked away, fast enough to show his anger. Within a few hundred yards he'd blended into the shadows along the sidewalk again, making him hard to see, a dark shape moving in and out of the darker patches along the sidewalk. The only reason she could see that much was because of the clarity spell she'd swept over her eyes earlier. Otherwise, it would have looked like he'd disappeared.

"Not sure that went very well," she murmured, mostly to herself and Boo. "Definitely didn't settle anything."

"Except for the stakes," Rhys answered. "No pun intended."

Despite the fact that the moment was too serious for it, she chuckled. She liked a good pun. "That life or death business? Is he threatening to kill you? Or just warning you that other lives are on the line, like his own had been?"

"A little of both," Rhys said. "We've managed this long without him killing me. But our…alliance is strained sometimes. His nighttime nature, the vampiric element is a lot craftier and mean. We're still brothers, but I think I might be the only one who thinks of that relationship as it once was. Virgil uses those feelings. But I don't know that he…*sees* me as a brother anymore."

"I'm sorry," she murmured again, glancing at the side of his face. They'd both been staring at the place where Virgil had disappeared. "And if you need to stay away from the café to be safe, I understand. I'll miss one of my best customers of course." She was trying to joke but it sounded awkward and flat.

"Just a customer, huh?" He turned and caught her gaze.

"I don't want you to get hurt," she said. Admitting to a crush right now felt selfish.

"Are you going to banish me from the café for my own good?" he asked.

"No. You're a grown man. You can make your own decisions. But I won't make things worse or try to influence that decision. It's up to you."

"And if I make things worse?"

"How would you do that?"

He stepped very close, so that he was looking a little down at her and she had to just tilt her head back a bit to keep holding his gaze. "Nina, I don't just come to the café for the good coffee and croissants."

That made her stomach do the fluttery dance. Her pulse bounded a little harder and she was glad there wasn't a vampire around to hear that anymore. She wasn't sure what to say to his declaration after just insisting she wouldn't complicate his decision by admitting to her feelings. But she suspected her shaky breath and the way her attention dropped to his mouth probably gave her away.

Boo chose that moment to bump against her leg. Hard. Hard enough to shover her a step away from Rhys. She glared down at the big cat. He was as big as a medium sized dog, but he rarely used that size for much of anything these days. The shove was unusual. When she glared at him, he meowed loudly. A warning sound. Then he bumped his head against her leg again.

"I think your cat wants us to keep our distance," Rhys said, also looking down at Boo.

"I think he's interfering where he wasn't asked."

Boo had the temerity to sit on the sidewalk and lick his paw as if he wasn't an interfering nag.

"He's right, though," Rhys said.

She glanced back up at him.

"I need to think clearly about all this. Before things get too complicated."

He was right. She knew he was right. She wasn't happy about the fact that he was right. But probably later she would be.

"Okay. You do what you need to do." She forced a smile. "The café will be here when you're ready." She almost said the "if" out loud but couldn't bring herself to open the possibility that he might never come back. She just didn't want to put those words into the universe.

He raised his hand a little, then made a fist and shoved both hands into the pockets of his jeans.

"Have a good afternoon," he said, trying to smile. He glanced down at Boo and gave him a little nod, then walked away, going in the opposite direction of his brother.

Nina watched him until he was a block away, before finally turning back to the coffee shop. She couldn't watch him disappear around a corner. That would feel too final. This way, she could maintain the illusion that he'd come back. That things could continue as they had been.

That she hadn't just watched Rhys Witherby walk away for the last time.

Two weeks passed without Rhys returning to the café. Two weeks was a long time. Since she'd opened her doors, he hadn't gone two full weeks without coming in at least once, even for a coffee to go. He'd told her, early on, that he worked in the neighborhood. Which meant avoiding the café would take effort.

The avoidance had to be deliberate.

He wasn't coming back.

By the second Saturday, Nina accepted he'd made his choice. She couldn't begrudge him that decision. And really, she hadn't known him well enough for this level of sadness. She didn't want to call the feeling rejection, but it felt like rejection.

Yet, she did understand. Given his life, his brother, and his sense of protectiveness, she knew he'd made the choice to avoid the café as a way to protect her. Not just to keep his brother from killing him. Although, honestly, that would have been a perfectly excellent reason for him to stay away, too. She didn't want him killed.

Whatever his reasoning, the result was the same. He wasn't coming back to the café. And whatever budding… whatever had been happening there was not going to happen. She needed to get her head out of the clouds and get back to work. She had a business to run.

Fortunately, Akira was back, so Nina left a lot of the customer attention to Akira while Nina made coffees and teas and dished up pastries and stayed behind the counter, pretending to clean and do paperwork. As it was Saturday, things were busy, but not as busy as the last two weekends.

That gave her a little too much time to think, which was bad, but it also meant she didn't feel guilty leaving so much for Akira to handle.

When the mid-afternoon lull meant there was nothing keeping Akira or Nina occupied, Nina took a break and headed into the bookstore. The owner was off that day but her second was behind the register, ringing up a couple of young women who had stacks of books between them. That made Nina smile.

She disappeared into the stacks, losing herself in looking at some new titles, reading blurbs, admiring some of the pretty covers. She picked out a new Mystery—she was a little too tender for a Romance—and took it up to the counter. It wasn't an answer, but the new novel would keep her brain occupied tonight so she didn't wallow. For some reason, she felt like if she could get through today, the day that marked two full weeks, she'd be okay.

After buying her book, she took a walk around the block, enjoying the fall sunshine. She finally returned to the café feeling somewhat refreshed and a lot less heartsore. Boo had remained in his usual spot on the too-small stool by the register all day, so she gave him a little scratch on the way past.

He rumbled a purr and then did a little cough thing that was unusual enough she frowned down at him. He stretched, his upper body hanging off the stool and his paws reaching behind her. She continued to frown down at him when he flopped again.

"You okay?" she murmured quietly.

Boo met her gaze and then stretched again, lengthening his entire upper body and his legs very far out in front of him.

She followed his reaching paw, looking across the café in the direction he was pointing.

To see Rhys sitting in his usual spot by the window, a coffee in front of him as he stared out the window.

She set her book behind the counter, replaced her apron, and crossed the café to join him. "Can I get you a muffin? A croissant maybe?" she asked, unable to resist a grin.

He looked up at her, his brown eyes sparking, his expression relaxed. "The coffee is good for now. Thanks."

"So." She stuffed her hands in the pockets of her apron. Feeling both awkward and delighted to see him again. "You're back."

"I'm back."

"To say goodbye or…?"

"Back to stay," he said quietly.

Her heartbeat started that ridiculous thumping again and her stomach did the fluttery dance.

He glanced at the cushioned seat across from him. "Have time for a break?"

She glanced back at Akira who was grinning at her. Boo also seemed to be grinning, though it was hard to tell as he'd curled back up and had his eyes closed, pretending to sleep.

Nina faced Rhys again. "I can take a few minutes to talk."

She settled in the seat across from him

He smiled at her.

He had a really great smile.

SAM AND BECKY AT
THE CAFÉ

SAM AND BECKY

Sam settled at a table near the window of the small, comfortable café attached to a cozy bookstore, feeling neither comfortable or cozy himself. The cushioned chairs and small wooden table holding his steaming mug of black coffee should have been more relaxing. That's the reason he wanted this to take place at a coffee shop, someplace neutral and yet easy to be.

But his nerves wouldn't allow him to relax.

This was the first time he'd seen Becky since they'd lost her brother, Denis to a car accident two years ago. He'd promised Denis he'd look after Becky, make sure she was always safe, had a big brother figure in her life to take care of her. And Sam had failed that promise spectacularly. For two years.

He wasn't sure he could forgive himself for that lapse,

but he had to try and at least make things up to Becky. Had to try and…start over with her.

Scanning the café as he waited for her, half wondering if she'd even show up after all this time, he decided the café had been a very good choice. There was a giant Maine coon sprawled on a stool that was much too small for him near the register. The woman behind the counter seemed nice and hummed as she cleaned the espresso machine. There were a handful of customers scattered around the seating area. A man near the back pounding away at a laptop, his drink ignored beside him on the small wooden table. An older woman drinking what appeared to be tea at one of the central tables that had firmer wooden chairs, reading a book—Sam couldn't see the cover so he wasn't sure what book. There was another couple of women sitting to one side of the café near the large opening that led into the bookstore, their heads together, deep in conversation. And three older men who looked like construction workers sitting around a table in the corner, all reading things on their phones as they sipped their drinks.

Light music drifted in from the adjacent bookstore, and he could see a few people moving around over there too. Becky liked bookstores, she'd always been a big reader—or used to be anyway—which was one of the reasons he'd picked this place. He figured if things went badly, he could always buy her a bunch of books as an apology and then get out of her life again.

Really, he just wanted to apologize. For fucking up. And then for disappearing. Once he'd done that, he'd abide by her wishes. If she'd allow him back in her life, he'd be there for her, as he'd promised her brother. The *way* he'd promised her brother. If she didn't want him back in her life, he'd disappear again and honor her request. That she'd even agreed to this meeting left him humbled. He'd half expected her to refuse. And he would have honored that, too. She didn't have to hear his apology. She didn't have to accept it after he offered. But he was grateful she'd at least hear it. That was more than he deserved.

The bell over the café door ran. He looked over anxiously, but it was a young mother shuffling two kids into the coffee shop. The woman glanced around, looking harried, then went directly to the counter where the barista immediately got her drinks and some crayons and coloring books for the kids. The small family settled at one of the tables with a couch and the two kids started immediately coloring and drinking their apple juice while the mother leaned back into the couch and took a deep breath that looked like relief.

Sam smiled to himself. But the little tableau made him think of Denis. Growing up, Denis had been the one who'd wanted a family, kids, that sort of comfortable chaos. He'd loved kids and wanted a partner who loved them too, and then he wanted to settled down and have a few. Living that settled sort of family life.

Sam hadn't been that guy. And had only barely understood why Denis might want something like that. Especially when there was so much of the world to see and so much to do. To Sam, settling down with kids and a wife had felt like giving up on all the adventures out there. It was one of the few things they hadn't had in common. Denis didn't want to travel the world and see everything there was to see. Sam didn't want to get stuck at home without ever having seen anything.

Well, he'd seen things now. Spent the last two years backpacking around the world, teaching where he could to make money to fund more travel. And in the end, he was right back home. But this time, to try and fix a mistake and a broken promise.

Someone cleared their throat and Sam looked away from the small family, though he hadn't actually been looking at them for several minutes, lost in his own thoughts about the past and his best friend. He blinked up at the person standing over him, thinking it would be the barista. He felt like he'd taken a hit to the side of his head when he realized it was Becky.

Seeing her again after two years took him all the way back in time. To the last time he'd seen her. Soft and sad and lovely. Her full lips trembling as she looked up at him with her big brown eyes. Trusting him. Grief tracking tears down her cheeks. Mutual sorrow and longing drawing them close together. That image superimposed itself on the present, a strange mental trick that stole his breath. Hit him with a gut punch of shame and guilt and other feelings he'd been trying to put behind him for two years.

She looked both the same and a little different now. Her thick brown hair was shorter—she'd worn it very long the last time they'd met. She was still breath-takingly pretty, but her features had sharpened into striking cheekbones and an elegant jawline. It was a slight change but still startling after only two years. Her full, heart-shaped mouth hadn't changed at all, though she was wearing lipstick today, and that mouth still caught way too much of his attention.

He gave himself a mental smack across the face and scrambled up from his seat.

"Hi," he said, then felt like an idiot. He'd imagined this moment for the last two years and still didn't have any more to offer her than "hi?" He gestured to the seat across from him. "Thanks for coming. I… I wasn't sure you would."

She shrugged, her expression calm and neutral. "It's been a long time since I heard from you. I figured it must be important." She gave him a small smile. "Let me just get a coffee and I'll be right back."

"Let me get that for you. I invited you here."

"It's okay," she said. "I can get my own drink."

She turned her back on him before he could do more, and he let her go. He was already making a mess of this. All the various ways he'd imagined this reunion, and he still didn't have the words. Not after seeing her again after so long.

Especially when seeing her still caused that desperate heat in his blood and made his heart thump harder. Fucking hell. She was his best friend's sister. His *dead* best friend. Who'd asked him to look after her. Two years later, he still couldn't be the person Denis had needed him to be.

This was probably a mistake. He couldn't do what Denis had asked him to do. Couldn't be a big brother type to Becky. He didn't *want* to have that kind of relationship with her. And that was the problem. He wanted more. Had wanted more for years. But that wasn't what Denis had wanted. And now, here Sam was, breaking his promise all over again, despite coming here to fix his past mistakes.

He should have just stayed away. Should have just let this go. Kept his distance and admitted that he'd failed his best friend. At least if he'd stayed away, he could have honored a part of Denis's request.

If he'd stayed away, he wouldn't be watching his best friend's sister with a desire that had apparently only gotten worse over the last two years. If he'd stayed away, he could pretend this need, this *hunger*, was behind him.

If he'd stayed away, he wouldn't now be terrified he'd hurt her all over again.

This had been a selfish move. A stupid move. Seeing her again hadn't settled anything. And apologizing wasn't going to assuage his guilt.

Because he still desperately wanted his best friend's sister.

***

Becky forced herself up to the counter at a slow and easy pace, attempting to appear unfazed by all of this. Calm. Self-assured. Unbothered. Not falling apart inside because she'd missed Sam so much it ached and seeing him again upended her entire world.

Wouldn't do for him to know that part.

No. She couldn't admit that to him. Not after all this time.

Two years was more than enough to get over a girlhood crush on her brother's best friend. She should be over him by now. She definitely wanted him to *think* she was over him now. Certainly didn't want him to know she still felt like a fool and hated the way things had ended after the last time they'd seen each other.

She hadn't regretted what happened between them. She hated the *way* things had happened.

But she had no intention of talking about that today. He'd called her out of the blue, asked to meet, and she'd said yes. He wanted to talk about something, she'd let him do the talking. She figured it had something to do with Denis. If it didn't, if it had to do with the last time they saw each other, she'd deal with that in the moment.

Please don't let him apologize for it, though. She might scream if he tried to apologize.

The barista narrowed her eyes as she handed Becky her mug of coffee with milk. "You okay?" she asked, her gaze jumping to Sam then back to Becky.

"Fine." Becky gave a nod she hoped appeared confident.

"First date?" the barista asked.

"Old family friend." Sam would never date her. She was his best friend's little sister. He'd made that perfectly clear by disappearing for two years after Denis's funeral.

"Ah." The woman's gaze jumped to Sam and back to Becky again. "Well, if you need anything, just wave. I'll come right over. More coffee. Cookies. An excuse to leave…"

Becky grinned, a real one this time. "Thank you. It'll be fine. Just… Bit of an emotional reunion is all."

"Fair enough. Maybe just the cookies then."

"Actually…" Becky ordered a giant chocolate chip cookies, which the barista handed her on a plate and waved away payment.

"My treat," she said. "I'm Nina, by the way. If you need me." She nodded to the giant gray cat sprawled on a tall stool that was clearly too small for him. "This is Boo. He'll help if you need it, too."

The cat in question lifted his head, yawned—which displayed a lot of tiny sharp teeth—stretched his front legs, somehow without falling off the stool, and then curled up again and closed his pale blue eyes.

Becky chuckled. "Real watch dog, isn't he?"

"More than you might expect from that display," Nina said.

Becky carried her coffee and cookie back to the table where Sam waited, his gaze turned out the window. He faced her suddenly, though, while she was still a few feet away, and the impact of his direct gaze left her mouth dry and her knees wobbly.

She hated that he still did that to her with just a look. The man's eyes should be illegal. Deep brown with a line around the edge that was nearly black. Lashes to die for. And heavy brows that somehow made him look *more* handsome instead of too rough. Strong jaw, perfect mouth… Everything about him was suited to her taste. She'd even dated men in college simply because they looked a little bit like Sam. None of them had been Sam of course. And she'd felt like an idiot every single time—after she realized what she'd done.

Straightening her spine, she covered the rest of the space between them with as much calm confidence as she could muster. When he suddenly stood and waited for her to sit across from him, she even managed to force a small smile.

"Really? Standing? Doesn't that seem…a bit old fashioned. Especially for people who've known each other as long as we have."

He sank back into his seat. "Habit," he said with a shrug. "My mother was strict about those kinds of things."

His mother had been strict about a lot of things. That was why he hung out at their house so much when they were younger. He could relax and just be himself there. In his own home, his mother had held him to a standard no child could ever meet.

"How's Vera doing?" she asked to be polite and to keep the small talk going. The longer they talked about nonsense, the longer she could pretend he wasn't about to apologize for something she didn't want him to apologize for.

"Fine. Busy with her clubs and groups and things. The usual." He didn't smile, and he didn't meet her gaze as he shrugged off the topic of his mother. "How have you been?"

"Great," she said. "Started my residency in April."

He smiled then, the first real smile he'd flashed since she'd entered the café and that expression broke her heart open, stole her breath, all the clichés. Of all the things about Sam that had made her swoon, his eyes and that smile were the two things that got to her the most.

"Pediatrician. Denis would be so proud."

"Yeah," she said with a misty smile. "He'd be really ridiculous about it all."

"Yeah he would. And the amount of bragging would have been embarrassing."

"Oh my god, yes." She chuckled and shook her head. Realized an instant later that moment of relaxed memory sharing had felt natural. Perfect and easy.

And painful.

"I miss him," she said. "Still. A lot."

"Me too."

In the silence that followed that admission, Becky scooped up the cookie and took a big bite. It was warm, the chocolate melty on her tongue, sweat and delicious without being too sugary. The cookie went perfectly with her milky coffee and she let out a little sigh at just how yummy it was.

When she looked up, Sam was staring at her. His look intent and steady. A wave of embarrassment washed through her, though she wasn't sure why. Maybe because she'd made such a big deal about a cookie.

She dropped her gaze and shrugged, trying to pretend she wasn't blushing. "Good cookie," she said, and winced at the defensiveness in her voice.

"Only got one?"

"I'm not buying you a cookie." Not that she'd paid for this one either. "You want a cookie, you have to get your own. But I do highly recommend them."

He chuckled. This time the tone was low, deep, the kind of chuckle that made her all hot and bothered, sent tingles along her spine. Damn it. She didn't want to react to him that way. Not after what had happened between them. He'd made clear where he stood. She needed to be okay with that and move on. *Should* have moved on. Two years. It had been two years! Getting all tingly and lusty for him after all that time was as foolish as her childhood crush had been.

"Why are we here?" she asked suddenly. She needed to leave soon. Seeing him again was too much. She thought she'd been prepared, thought she'd put her feelings for him aside. She had not. And he was going to break her heart all over again if she weren't careful. "You haven't so much as emailed since after the funeral. What's this about?"

Sam dropped his gaze to his own coffee, but not before she saw his wince. Fuck. He felt guilty. This was his guilt and apology meeting. She'd been afraid of that. But he was his mother's son. Just like standing for her when she joined him, apologizing for a perceived wrong had been drilled into him from a young age. He'd feel like he owed her that apology. And even though it was late—two years late at that!—he'd still feel like he had to deliver the apology no matter what.

If he said the words, though, she really would scream.

That might be disruptive to the café and it would certainly bring Nina and maybe even her cat Boo running and she didn't want all that embarrassment.

So she decided to preempt the whole thing. She wasn't a kid who waited on Sam's every word anymore, and she wasn't going to stand for his apology now.

"If this is about…where we left things, what happened right before you left, forget about it. Do *not* attempt to apologize or I will throw my coffee at you. It's hot. You would not like that."

His mouth twitched, but whatever that twitch meant, he hid the response quickly. "Becky…"

"Nope. No. Not listening to it. If you're here to reminisce about Denis, we can do that. If you're hear because it's been two years and you feel like you have to check on me for Denis's sake, you have officially done that. I'm fine. As I said, started my residency. Have a nice apartment, with plants I've managed to keep alive. And when my residency is over and I can manage it without feeling like a neglectful pet parent, I'm getting a dog."

The mouth twitch this time turned into a soft smile. "You always wanted a dog."

"Damn straight. I'd get one now, but my work hours are absurd and it would be irresponsible."

"Are you… Are you dating anyone?"

"No time for dates right now."

"Anyone…" He twisted his mug between his hands. "Any ex's I should know about? Someone you want me to beat up since Denis isn't here to do the job?"

The comment startled a laugh from her. A genuine one. They'd both always threatened to beat up anyone she dated who didn't treat her well. She'd appreciated the backup even if she'd have never gotten them to do any such thing. It was just nice to know they had her back. And they had bought her ice cream and watched movies with her all night when she'd been dumped by her high school sweetheart right before the senior prom. She hadn't been very upset about that breakup. She'd been dating Sara in an attempt to forget about Sam. In her teenage brain, she'd even thought the alliteration would help with that. It had not. And so she wasn't particularly heartbroken when Sara dumped her for another girl with perfect hair. But she'd loved that her brother and his best friend had looked after her that night.

It was one of her favorite memories of the three of them together.

"No exes you need to beat up," she assured. "My last breakup was…six months ago. And we'd only been on about four dates before I ended things. So it's all good."

"Why?"

"Why what?"

"Why did you break up with them?"

Because he wasn't you. "Because I was too busy and he was too demanding of my time. We weren't suited."

"Fair enough."

"You have a girlfriend out there somewhere? Wife? Three beautiful kids and a house in Spain?"

He choked a little. "Three kids? In two years? Aren't you supposed to be a doctor?"

She shrugged. "There's such a thing as triplets. Or you could have adopted. Fallen in love with a young widow and taken on her kids? You never know."

"Your imagination," he said with another of those chuckles that made her skin tingle.

She ignored it. "So? No widow and three children in a villa in Thailand?"

He scowled a little. "How did they get from Spain to Thailand?"

"You've traveled a lot, right? That's what you left to do. Travel. I don't know where you might have fallen in love and settled down? Could be anywhere. I didn't want to make assumptions."

He didn't stop scowling, but he did say, "No wife and kids and no villas anywhere."

"Okay." She sipped her coffee.

"No girlfriend either."

"Fair enough."

"Hasn't been anyone serious in the last two years."

"Too busy moving countries. Got a girl in each port? That's a saying right."

"For sailors. Not backpackers."

"Well, I mean, wouldn't need to be a port, I suppose."

"No one, Becky. There's been no one." He stopped twisting his mug and met her gaze. "Fuck."

"What?" She straightened. "Are you going to try apologizing? Because we've already established that would be a bad idea."

"No. Not going to apologize. At least not to you. I might have to visit Denis and apologize to him."

"What for?"

"I promised him, in the hospital, right before…" He pulled in a deep breath. "I promised him I'd look after you. Make sure you were okay. Be…a brother to you when you needed one."

She rolled her lips into her mouth so she wouldn't

comment. But that admission hit hard in multiple ways. All of them heartbreaking.

Love and sadness that her brother had thought of *her* as he was dying. Guilt and grief wrapped all around that.

Tenderness and sympathy for Sam, making that deathbed promise to his best friend.

The heartbreak of knowing that was all Sam wanted from her. All he considered her. An obligation to his best friend. A "little sister" to look out for.

The love and anger she felt toward that sentiment in equal measure. Love, because he cared. Anger, because she wasn't his sister and didn't want to be his sister.

And a lot of annoyance at herself for allowing her childhood crush to continue breaking her heart.

"I fucked up my promise to Denis almost immediately," Sam said. He held her gaze still, didn't look away even though his words made her want to duck and hide. "And then I made things worse by leaving and cutting you out of my life. I thought… I thought I was doing the right thing at the time. For you. For what I'd promised Denis. I didn't think I could do what he asked of me while I was near you so I took the cowards way out and left."

"I told you I don't want an apology. It's done. You don't owe me anything. And Denis shouldn't have asked that of you anyway. I'm not your sister. You're not responsible for me."

"I know that."

"Good. Then we've said all that needs to be said and can go on with our lives. Leave the past behind us. All that." She waved a hand and broke eye contact first to drop her gaze to her coffee. She'd wrapped her hands around the mug, but couldn't feel the warmth seeping into her palms. Her whole body felt cold and the ache in her chest *hurt*. Hurt more than she'd thought possible.

After two years, after all the times she'd thought about what she might say to him if he showed back up in her life, the different conversations she'd played out… She'd have thought she'd be able to handle this. But she couldn't. She just couldn't. It was too much. Too hard. Too painful.

Because like it or not, she was still fucking in love with him.

She launched out of her seat, leaving the coffee mug and half eaten cooking on the table. "I have to go. Work. Good seeing you. Send me a postcard from your next stop, maybe? Or don't." She started to walk away, but he reached out and touched her hand, stopping her, freezing her in place.

His touch was gentle. She could have easily kept walking. He didn't even wrap his fingers around her hand. But the contact broke something inside her and she nearly dropped to her knees. The feel of his warm, callused fingers on her skin left her so shaken, she did sit down again, though with her back half to him.

He dropped the touch instantly, but kept his hand on the table, near her. Near enough she could have set her fingers into his if she'd wanted to.

"Please don't leave yet," he said quietly. "I know I haven't earned your time or patience with me. I know you don't owe me this meeting or this conversation. I half expected you to not show up after the way I behaved and I wouldn't have blamed you. But you're here now. And… And I don't want to end things badly this time."

She waved that way, though she couldn't look at him when she did. "Forget about it. It was a long time ago."

"Feels like just yesterday."

She sighed. Unfortunately, he was right. "You don't owe me anything either," she said. "Certainly not what…what Denis asked of you. I don't need another brother. I don't need you to replace him in my life."

"I couldn't do that anyway and wouldn't want to try."

"Good. Then… Then we're settled. No need to feel you've disappointed Denis or broken any promises. We're good."

"No," Sam said. "We're not. I've lied to you. I lied to Denis. And it's time I come clean."

She did turn to face him then, her eyes narrowed. "What did you do?"

He sighed, opened his palm on the table, glanced out the window before meeting her gaze again. "Probably the worst thing ever," he said. "I fell in love with you."

Sam held his breath. He wasn't sure what else to do after that confession. He hadn't meant to make it. But seeing her again had broken something in him, and he hadn't been able to hold it back. He'd been dishonest with her last time. He needed to be honest now.

But as the moments ticked past and she just stared at him, he realized this was one bit of truth he probably should have kept to himself. His feelings weren't her responsibility. He should have kept that shit to himself, ensured she was doing well, and then left the fucking café. Now they had this… thing hanging out there between them. His big old broken heart on full display. And he felt horrible for foisting that on her.

"Sorry," he said, when the silence finally got to him. "I… I should have kept that to myself. Obviously, I don't expect anything and I don't want you to feel like…like this is something you have to deal with. Right now, this was supposed to be about me finally honoring Denis's last wish, making sure your life was good, everything was good. I can't…I can't do the part where I treat you like a sibling." He huffed out a breath. "Obviously. But I… Shit." He ran a hand through his hair. "Just…sorry."

"If you say sorry one more time, I really will scream," she said, her voice tense and quiet.

It was on the tip of his tongue to apologize for apologizing so much but he swallowed that impulse. She didn't look happy and he had no doubt she meant her threat to scream.

He nodded, his gaze dancing away from her, toward the door. The bell overhead dinged as a new customer came in. He barely paid them any attention. "Okay. No more apologizing, but… I will go. You shouldn't have to deal with…me like this."

"If you stand up, I will never forgive you," she said, also

quietly, her voice barely audible over the sounds of the espresso machine starting.

"Becky…"

"Shut. Up." She looked up and met his gaze. "Do you have any idea what you've just done?"

He shrugged, not sure what to say. Especially after she'd told him to shut up. Doing that felt like the wiser move than trying to speak.

"I have been in love with you for as long as I can remember," she said quietly. "Most of my life, once I was old enough to recognize the emotion."

Suddenly Sam couldn't breathe very well. He fisted his hands in his lap, not sure where this was going, but terrified to even move.

"I spent years, *years,* trying to convince myself to move on from you. To let you go. You thought of me as a little sister, that was good enough. We could be friends. We had so many good memories of the three of us together. I didn't want to mess any of that up. So I tried *so hard* to stop loving you." She let out a sound that, on a good day, probably would have been a chuckle. Now it just sounded pained and tired. "Sam. You are such an idiot."

He couldn't really argue with that. He also still didn't know what to say. Apologies seemed the exact opposite of what she wanted from him in that moment. So he didn't speak, mostly for fear of putting his foot in his mouth again.

But…

Becky had loved him. Once upon a time. She'd been in love with him.

His throat dry, he did have one question to ask. "Did you still…feel this way after, after Denis. When we…"

"Yes," she said, without any hesitation. "I knew what happened between us was just…mutual comfort. We were both grieving, tired, sad. We both wanted to feel something else. Sex is good for that. Good for getting out of your own head. And I did not want to be in my head in that moment." Her gaze danced away. "I thought… I thought I had used you and that's why you left. That you were angry with me."

"There were two of us that night. You didn't *trick* me into anything." His hands curled into tighter fists so he forced himself to relax them. "I needed you that night as much as you needed me."

"But then you felt like you'd betrayed Denis."

"Yes. I did. He asked me to look after you like a brother, not fuck you within hours of his funeral."

She winced and Sam kicked himself for his tone. He opened his mouth to apologize again, then snapped it shut. He suspected she was still on the verge of screaming at him.

"I didn't mean that to come out that way," he did say. "Like I said, there were two of us that night."

"Did you…have these feelings for me that night? Or after? Or did that night enable you to stop loving me."

He should tell her he'd gotten over her and they could return to friends, move past all this. It's what Denis would have wanted. Probably what Becky needed. But he couldn't force himself to say the words.

So he just went with the truth. "I'd been in love with you before that night. And knew I was lying to Denis when I made my promise to him. Because I was in love with you and knew I would never be able to fully…act toward you the way he wanted me to." He started to reach for her hand, then stopped himself, leaving his fist bunched up at the edge of the table. "I left, because once we'd been together, I knew I was a goner. That I'd only make things worse because of my feelings. You turned to me for comfort. I was happy to give it. But that was all and I didn't want to hear you say that was all." He shrugged. "Selfish I guess. But there you are. When it comes to you, I am selfish."

"Meaning?"

"I want everything, Becky. I want your heart, your love. I want you in my life. Everyday for the rest of it. There's no one else and, despite trying not to love you, I still do. And I feel like a major asshole for burdening you with that. Especially if that girlhood crush you had that you thought was love has gone away. I shouldn't have said anything."

"You're about to get the rest of this cookie in your face for saying what you just did. Girlhood crush? Girlhood *crush*? How dare you. How dare you assume my feelings were so fleeting that would have faded away while yours remained strong. What do you take me for?"

"A beautiful, brilliant woman who deserves better than me."

"Oh shut up. What a nonsense line. What have you ever done that makes you unworthy of love?" She huffed. "I could just smack your mother for making you believe that."

"I fucked my best friend's sister right after his funeral when I'd promised to look after her."

"A woman you were in love with—according to you—and who was also in love with you at the time—even if I hadn't said so out loud. You didn't do anything *wrong*. Do you think I don't deserve love? That I'm somehow bad because I fucked my brother's best friend hours after his funeral? Am I a horrible person?"

"No! Of course not."

"Then neither are you. You are an idiot. But not a horrible person." She cursed under her breath. "Sam, damn it, I still love you. Okay. I'm still in love with you. That hasn't gone away even thought *I* tried to stop. So…" She made a face and looked away from him. "So you're just going to have to deal with that." Her head bobbed in a nod that looked suspiciously like she was trying not to cry.

If he made her cry in this moment, he'd never forgive himself. But he didn't know how to make the emotions stop either.

"Please don't cry," he murmured.

She sniffled. "I'm not."

"I don't know if it helps," he said, "or if this will make it worse, but…I'm still in love with you. I will be in love with you for the rest of my life."

"Well. That's just great. Where does that leave us now? I love you. You love me. We're both going to be in love forever. Now what?"

The irrational urge to smile took hold of him, and he had to quickly school his features. He wasn't sure how she'd react to his grin. But a light inside him turned on and he was certain it was shining out of his eyes. She looked so frustrated and distraught he just wanted to pull her onto his lap and hug her for the rest of the day. He wanted the right to tell her, over and over again, that he loved her. He wanted to make her *believe* him.

But to do that, he had a feeling that they had to start fresh.

Which meant no pulling her into his lap, no kissing her—yet—no reaching for her until she reached for him.

He said, "I have an idea, if you're willing to listen."

She sniffled again and nodded rapidly, blinking hard as she straightened and faced him.

"How about we start over. As the adults we are now. Without the guilt of the past. Or the stupid misunderstandings."

"How would we do that? We have all this history. I don't want to ignore that or let it go. Those are some of my best memories."

"Mine too," he said, turning his hand palm up on the table between them. When she slipped her fingers through his, their palms sliding against each other, he felt like his world was clicking back into place. Damage he hadn't realized was there knitted itself together. The start of healing. "I don't mean we forget our past. I mean, we reintroduce ourself. Go on a date."

A little laugh escaped her. "A date?" She shrugged and her hand tightened in his. "A date actually sounds really nice."

"And you can tell me all about medical school and your new residency. And I'll tell you all about my travels."

"Are you leaving again?"

He shook his head. "I'm getting my teaching certification as we speak. I've talked to a couple of principles who are hiring."

"You…planned on settling back here? Even before we talked?"

"I did." He sighed. "I messed up so much with you. And I wasn't making things right running away. So I decided to come back and make things right. Between us and between me and Denis."

"If we date, that definitely isn't living up to your promise to him."

"I think if he realized what we felt for each other all those years, he would have changed his request. He loved you so much. He wanted you happy."

"And you think you can make me happy?"

"I think we can try for happy together. I think we might just have a shot at it."

Her soft smile broke through and Sam felt something tight around his chest loosen. He'd missed that smile. He'd missed her.

"So," she said, leaning forward so her other arm rested on the table.

He mirrored her, leaning forward to. Her scent caught him, seeped into him, the memory of her melding with this new moment. This hopeful start. A faintly floral smell, though he'd never known which flower. This scent would always be her to him.

"So," she repeated. "Where should we go on our date?"

He looked around the café. "I suppose, if we wanted to,

we could count this as a start to a first date. Coffee. Maybe look around the bookstore. Then…dinner. Do you have work?"

"Not until tomorrow morning. Which means I do need an early night."

"Okay. Early dinner. Then I'll assure you get home in time to get enough sleep for your shift."

"Sleep?"

The thread of lust in her tone nearly undid him. He'd give just about anything to spend the night with her again. But this time, they were doing things the right way around. "Tonight. Yes. You have an early morning. But I'm not promising that I won't try and keep you up too late in the future."

"Good." She tightened her fingers around his and he tightened his hold on her hand. He didn't want to release her, ever. And he was just so grateful for being able to hold her even this way.

She glanced past him, toward the large opening into the bookstore. "You said something about books?"

He chuckled, watched the way color flowed over her cheeks even as she held his gaze, her smile mischievous and oh so Becky.

For the first time in two years, he felt the guilt and sorrow in his gut relax, felt himself sinking into this moment, with this woman. He loved her and she loved him. That was a hell of a start. And maybe, just maybe, Denis would have approved.

Because Sam was going to spend the rest of his life making sure Becky knew just how much she was loved.

KASSIDEY AT THE CAFÉ

KASSIDEY

Kassidey didn't like books. She tried to like books. Everyone liked books, right? What was wrong with books? They had stories. They occupied your brain for hours. They had great information sometimes. Okay, sometimes they had bad information. And sometimes they were written badly. But nothing was perfect. Like everything else, books were a spectrum from delightful and entertaining/informative to drivel that was only suited for propping open a door.

But Kassidey just…didn't like books. They creeped her out. The sound of the paper moving over paper made her skin crawl. The smell of paper and ink left her desperate for fresh air. The sight of all those shelves and the dust and the…life. Just not for her.

Well, she liked being alive. That was actually one of the reasons she didn't like books.

So having to meet her counselor at a café that was *right* next to a bookstore felt like a slap in the face. Veronica knew about the book thing. That was the reason Kassidey *had* a counselor. The book thing. And the wanting to be alive thing. It was like Veronica was *trying* to troll her.

To be fair, the café part of the establishment was pretty nice. Smelled like coffee and buttery pastries with chocolate undertones—couldn't even smell the books if she stayed close enough to the counter with the espresso machine. If she only looked out the large front windows to the busy sidewalk beyond, she didn't have to see the books. There were even tables, surrounded by cushioned couches and chairs that faced the café counter and ensured she had a hard time seeing through the giant opening into the bookstore. With just the right angle, she could *almost* pretend the bookstore wasn't *right there*.

Except she could still *feel* all those books. Just sitting there. Waiting.

Kassidey shivered and scooped up her coffee mug with two hands. She'd picked a latte because she didn't think her gut could handle black coffee or anything without milk. But maybe she should have gone for a soothing tea. Between the books and her nerves, her gut was churning. And she worried even the delicious, foamy latte wouldn't settle well.

She scanned the coffee shop, careful not to look to far to her left in case she spotted the books, and took in the clientele while waiting on Veronica. She was always waiting for Veronica. Felt like every time they met, she had to wait for Veronica. And the fact that Veronica was making her wait this close to a bookstore was deliberate.

And a little mean.

There weren't a lot of people scattered around the café at the moment. An older woman sitting at one of the tables in the center of the seating area, drinking a steaming cup of something Kassidey thought might be tea based on the shape of the mug. The woman was reading a book, so Kassidey didn't look at her too long because it meant looking at a book. There was another man, middle aged, with his head bent over his laptop as he typed. He looked up once, his gaze turned inward and his mouth moved, then he returned to his computer again. Near the front of the café, at the big window, a handsome man sat in one of the couches, flipping through a magazine, and drinking from one of the large cappuccino mugs, an empty plate on the low table in front of him.

The barista behind the counter occasionally glanced at the handsome man, and he occasionally glanced at her, but they weren't speaking. Something interesting there, Kassidey thought. And if she wasn't here to meet Veronica and there wasn't a bloody bookstore *right there*, she'd probably enjoy watching the two of them.

Beside the register, on a tall stool, sprawled a pale gray cat. She wasn't sure what kind of cat but he was obviously too large for the stool, had tufted, pointed ears, and looked to be sleeping, though Kassidey did catch him opening his eyes to scan the surroundings, before letting them drift shut again.

She wondered as much about the cat as she did the barista

and the handsome man at the window, and the cat was easier to watch. The barista had called him Boo. Good name for a pale gray cat. There was something soothing about the way he sprawled willy nilly on the stool, like it didn't matter that he spilled over the edges and his position looked pretty precarious. He was comfortable and no one was going to move him. Kassidey liked that.

A shadow fell over her, blocking the cat, and Kassidey looked up to see Veronica standing over her, smiling her careful, professional smile.

"Kassidey," she greeted. "Sorry to make you wait. I was just next door in the bookstore and got distracted."

Kassidey didn't smile back and she didn't rise to the bait Veronica had just tossed out. She simply blinked up at her and waited for her to take her seat.

"Is the coffee good?" Veronica asked as she sat in the cushioned seat across the low table.

"Delicious."

"You realize I picked this place on purpose."

"I do."

"You can be around books without it killing you, Kassidey."

"Tell that to my lizard brain."

"I am."

"Is this a test?"

"Maybe."

"What happens if I pass? Do I get to go back to my life finally?"

"We both know that's not going to happen the way you want it to. Not after all this time."

"I hate books."

"I know." Veronica set a reusable black tote bag on the floor next to her seat, which Kassidey figured was full of books, and rose again. "I'll be right back. I need a drink."

Kassidey continued to sip her own drink as she waited. To be fair, the latte really was delicious. Would be even better if it settled in her stomach, though.

She flicked a glance at the bag next to Veronica's seat. Looked away. Stared at the cat so she could ignore the bag.

When Veronica sat, Kassidey decided not to wait. Veronica would just talk about the things Kassidey didn't want to discuss. "Are the papers signed finally?"

"No. Not yet."

Kassidey growled. "What now?"

"They want to negotiate one last point."

"We've been negotiating points for three years. I've already told them they could have all of it. What more do they want?"

"It has to do with the handover."

"I'm starting to think you're a crap lawyer."

"Best you'll get," Veronica said without an ounce of offense.

Kassidey wouldn't have minded her taking offense. She was the one who'd chosen a place by a bookstore after all.

"They want to ensure they don't…fall into the same trap you did at the hand off."

Kassidey lifted her lip in a snarl. Of course. Because of

course *they* knew. She wasn't allowed to keep the information to herself. Which she absolutely would have. The person she'd inherited from certainly had.

It wasn't fair she had to go through three years of this to pass off the inheritance that had taken her a month to receive. A month when she'd been blissfully ignorant and hadn't actually disliked all books yet. She hadn't been a book person. She had been pretty neutral on them actually. Neither hated nor loved. They were there. She wasn't a reader, so she didn't collect them or anything. But she hadn't actively avoided all places with collections of books five years ago.

Now, she really couldn't stand being in the same place as books.

"What's in the bag if it's not the final contract?" she asked. She'd already guessed but she was feeling pissy.

"I bought a few novels next door." Veronica met her gaze over her coffee—black, Kassidey noted. Someone's gut wasn't at them at least. "And, believe it or not, I brought the contract. It isn't signed yet. You'll have to approve the single change they made. Then we can sign."

"Wait. Really? After all this time, this one change means they will definitely sign and it's not just a continued stalling tactic?" Because she was afraid to hope that was the case. The new couple inheriting had known from the start what they'd be getting into and had been stalling the transfer for years. Too long for Kassidey. She was never meant to be in possession of the library for this long.

She had not an ounce of magical skill that gave her control of all those magic books. Which meant the books were the ones in control of her. And she *hated* it. She had to be around them regularly. She had no choice. Forced into the library to balance the stupid books or something. Because of the way she'd inherited, because it was sudden and she was supposed to be a temporary holder until the real owners finally showed up. Like an executor of a will or something. Except the people who were really supposed to inherit the place didn't show up for two whole years.

And they understood what the library was, what it meant to be responsible for it, so they'd been stalling. Avoiding taking the reins for as long as possible.

Which left Kassidey stumbling along, forced monthly into that cacophony of books, all the noise and stinging magic and smells and color. She could *feel* them sucking the life out of her to feed their own lives. Because she wasn't the one that was supposed to be there.

She just wanted her life back. And she never wanted to see another book ever again.

"The final clause is…complicated, though," Veronica said. "You might not want to sign it."

"Tell me." She knew it had been a bad idea to get her hopes up. Veronica wasn't actually a crap counselor. She was an excellent one. But also one of the few who understood what was at stake, which made it really impossible for Kassidey to replace her even if she had been crap at her job. One of the few other lawyers who understood all this was representing the other side.

"They want to delay the handover for six more months."

"What? No! Don't they get how…awful this has been for me? Are they just trying to torture me?"

"No. It's just that Quin is pregnant and they're both afraid if they take over the library this month, it will affect her pregnancy."

"She was not pregnant three years ago," Kassidey growled. "They could have also waited to get pregnant until they'd taken over and stabilized the place."

Veronica shrugged. "A stalling tactic," she agreed. "And a mean one at that. There's a reason we have avoided being in the same room with them during this negotiation. You would not like them."

"I don't have to like them. I just have to hand off their proper inheritance and get it out of my hair."

"Six more months and they've said they will take it. Finally."

"But then what? At six months they'll say they have a baby. And then she'll get pregnant again. Or they'll claim they can't with a kid period and can I hold onto the place for another eighteen years. I cannot. It is not designed for me. It's not a place I can take care of. I've been doing it too long already. And if I keep doing it, it will kill me or make me insane." She leaned forward and set her mug down, then rested her forearms on her knees as she stared up at Veronica. "I want my life back, V. You have got to help me here."

"I knew the timeline wouldn't work for you," she said. "But I had to make you the offer. They've claimed they'll sign tomorrow if you agree to the extra six months."

"But will they? They've said that before. And yet we're still doing this. Don't I have any way to force their hand?"

Veronica considered her quietly for a long moment, still sipping at her black coffee, but her dark eyes were speculative and intent. She was thinking hard. Kassidey had seen that look before. It could be good or bad for Kassidey, that look. And she wanted to rush Veronica with questions. But she kept her mouth shut and waited.

Finally, Veronica said, "The one thing that might work is you pulling back from the negotiations and saying you won't pass the library on to them now. Period."

"What? How would that work? I don't want to keep the place. And they are obviously reluctant to take it or they wouldn't have stalled me for three years."

"Reluctant does not mean they don't want it. They do. How could they not? It represents a great deal of power for them, even if it isn't anything you can access. They are stalling but they don't want to lose out on the library. If you threaten to just keep it, to end all the negotiation and keep the library for yourself, they might panic and hurry things up."

Kassidey leaned back and took a deep breath. Could she risk that? "What if they accept and walk away? What if they're relieved to be off the hook?"

She hadn't met the couple face-to-face. She had no idea of their real character, only what she learned through Veronica and their lawyer—who she had met. She wasn't sure if they'd call her bluff and leave her high and dry. And in life-long possession of a library she had no business being in charge of.

"It's a risk," Veronica admitted. Which Kassidey had to respect. One thing Veronica did not do was blow smoke up Kassidey's skirt. "But if we don't take that risk now, you're right about what they might do six months from now. Even if they sign the revised contract, they'll ensure there's an addendum in there that allows for renegotiation before the contract terms are finalized."

"And I'd have to sign that if I wanted to get them to sign."

Veronica nodded.

"I think I might hate these people."

"Another reason their counsel and I both thought it best for you all not to meet in person."

"What would we say? How do we try this bluff? And what happens if it backfires? All the details. I can't make this decision without them."

"Fair." Veronica smiled. "That's something I like about you."

"Yeah, well, it was a hard-won trait." One she hadn't possessed five years ago and should have. Digging for and insisting on the details and loopholes and possible issues might have saved her all this time. But then, she hadn't had Veronica to advise her back then. She might not have even understood the details, even if she'd asked for them.

"Here are the options," Veronica said. "We bluff. Say you are not going to sign away the library anymore. That the library is in your possession and obviously the rightful inheritors no longer want it, so you're keeping it."

Even the idea made Kassidey shiver, but she nodded. "Go on."

"They can go one of two ways in their response. One, they'll be overjoyed, call our bluff, and you'll be stuck with the library until the next heirs come along."

"Which might not be for years."

"Which might not be for decades."

Fuck. "What's the second response?"

"They panic, assume you're not bluffing, and demand the library immediately be passed to them as the rightful heirs."

"Which you will make me not do for a bit longer."

"Which I will counsel you not to do for another few weeks. Just to draw things out." Veronica shrugged. "They deserve a little of what they've put you through for the last three years."

Okay. Veronica wasn't so bad. Even if she had picked a café next to a bookstore.

Kassidey took a deep, sighing breath and stared at Boo the cat on his too-small stool for a solid minute before saying, "Which do you think it'll be? You've met them. Will they respond with option one or option two?"

"I wouldn't advise this tactic if I didn't think it would work. They want this library. But they know the consequences of accepting it, what happens once they do. They're using you to keep it in a state of suspension until they *want* to accept it. They are not terribly concerned for the consequences to you. As your counsel, I am."

"Then why did you bring us to a café next to a bookstore?"

"Because not all books are the library you've inherited. And because the woman who runs this place is a witch. It's a safe place to discuss such things."

Kassidey blinked at that. Then looked back at the barista and her seemingly-asleep cat. She was a witch? Did that mean the cat was more than a cat? Or just a cat?

"The books here aren't magic books… Well, outside of the magic of losing yourself in another world. Some of them are fantasies, of course, so there's that. But they aren't the books that are sucking your life away. Your lizard brain may not ever be able to read a book for pleasure again, but it needs to know not all books are the library books."

"You're my counselor not my counselor. My mental health is someone else's concern."

Veronica huffed out a laugh. "When you get a proper therapist, then I'll stop pushing you. And, after this, you should get into counseling. With someone who understands the consequences of excess exposure to magic."

"I'll consider that once this is done."

"Fair enough. So what's your decision?"

"I don't want this to drag on for another six months. And I certainly don't want it pushed past that. I think it's worth the risk."

"And if I'm wrong and they wash their hands of their inheritance?"

"Then I guess I'm screwed and I learn how to live with it."

"Good answer." Veronica stood, holding her now empty mug in one hand and the black tote bag in the other. "I'll get back to you in a couple of days. We can meet here again to discuss the outcome."

"Not your office?" Kassidey tried not to look over her shoulder at the bookstore, but she could still feel all those books, living there. It didn't matter what Veronica said, those books still felt like living things and she just did not like it.

"Not my office." Veronica's mouth flattened. Then she said, "I think their lawyer has the place bugged. He wouldn't have this place bugged, though. They all know how you feel about books. That was the other reason I picked this particular coffee shop."

"You could have explained that from the beginning."

"What would be the fun in that?"

Veronica carried her mug back up to the counter and said goodbye to the barista, giving Boo the cat a head scritch on the way out. Boo took the scratch happily, then glanced back at Kassidey, his pale blue eyes steady on her for a full thirty seconds, before he closed them and once again went to sleep —or seemed to.

So. A witch's café. A bookstore. And a cat that was probably more than a cat.

Five years ago, all of this would have been very unbelievable to her. Now... For some reason, it was comforting. Not the bookstore part. But at least the café was nice.

They met in the same café a week later. Kassidey still didn't like all the books so close. She wasn't getting over her dislike of books any time soon. But being in the café was a kind of relief. She even gave Boo a scritch herself before finding a table in the back where she wouldn't have to look at the bookstore.

Veronica was, as usual, a little late. But Kassidey waited patiently. She and Veronica had only spoken briefly during in the week. And Veronica hadn't revealed the real heirs' reaction to Kassidey pulling out of the negotiation. She'd only learn how they'd responded today.

In the intervening week, though, Kassidey had considered the consequences of this negotiation tactic, and what happened if it backfired on them. What happened if she got stuck with the library until the next heir came along? That could take decades. She wasn't sure her mental health would stand up to that kind of consequence. But maybe she could find help. Someone who knew more about magic libraries and how to stabilize them. Veronica might even be able to help her find that help.

Because if the worst happened, then it happened, and she'd live with that. Anything to get out of this limbo. This half-life of waiting and dealing and barely managing while she waited. If she had to hold the library for another few decades, then she'd learned how to do that instead of just holding on by her fingernails hoping it was all over soon. She'd figure it out and deal with it.

Once she'd come to that conclusion, the response of the heirs mattered a lot less. She was prepared for either end now. And walking away from the table was absolutely an option.

Which meant she was in a pretty decent mood when Veronica finally sat down across from her, black coffee in hand. The black tote bag settled on the floor near her feet. She hadn't been in many good moods around Veronica, so her chipper greeting was met with suspicion.

"Are you okay?" Veronica asked. "What's happened? What's wrong?"

Kassidey chuckled. "Nothing. I've just come to terms with the worst-case scenario for our tactic. If they tap out, I have a plan to get through the next few decades."

"Really?"

"I haven't let myself have those thoughts until this last week. I never allowed myself to plan for the heirs *not* taking the library. I was afraid to. But forcing myself to face that this week has actually been really helpful. I'll manage. No matter their response."

Veronica smiled. "I'm delighted to hear that."

"Because they're washing their hands of the library?"

"No. Because they're desperate to re-initiate negotiations and are angry that you're trying to keep 'their' library."

Kassidey snort-laughed. "Yeah. They're the victims here."

"My exact feelings. So. Since they're all in a panic now and desperate to get things moving again, we're going to ignore them for a full month. This is why I'm glad to hear you're settled into the idea of holding the library a bit longer. A month will give them time to stew. And by the time we come back to the table, we'll be in a great position. Not only to get the library passed off, but to ensure your time as executor of the estate is properly compensated."

"Wait. What?"

"You should be paid, and paid handsomely, for the time, effort, and difficulty this situation has imposed on you. They are very wealthy people. And we'll negotiate a sufficient payment to ensure the last five years were worth it." Veronica winked. "Including enough for that counseling you need."

"Ha!" Kassidey laughed. Then laughed again. Shaking her head. "You really are very good at your job."

"Yes. Yes I am." Veronica sipped her coffee serenely.

"So in a month's time, I'll be rid of the library *and* likely set up financially. At least for a while."

"Precisely. As a warning, do not allow them to contact you directly. If they try, redirect them to me. Trust me. I'll ensure we get you everything you deserve. In a good way."

Kassidey let out a breath and felt the stirring of tears tickling her eyes, tightening the back of her throat. She was going to have a life again. She'd be able to move on. And the library would no longer be sucking the life out of her.

"Thanks," she said. "Thank you for everything."

"That'll teach you not to doubt my machinations," Veronica said, though her eyes looked a bit bright and damp, too.

"Coffee's on me."

"Deal." Veronica glanced past her toward the bookstore, and raised her brows. "Too soon?"

"Too soon," Kassidey said. But... Maybe someday.

Maybe she'd be able to sit by, even go into, a bookstore again. Not yet. She still disliked books a great deal.

But someday.

And until then, she'd enjoy this café and its delicious coffee and its strange giant cat currently grinning at her from his too-small stool by the register.

She gave him a little solute with her coffee mug. Then settled into a planning session with Veronica, finally seeing the light at the end of the five-year tunnel. And that light looked good and bright.

CARY AND DEACON AT THE CAFÉ

CARY AND DEACON

Cary Redmond pushed through the glass door and grinned at the cute café, the smells of brewing coffee settling deep into her coffee-addicted soul. This was the best possible thing she could imagine. A coffee shop attached to a bookstore.

"There's a bookstore," she excitedly whispered to Deacon.

"Yes," he said, his expression neutral, though she spotted the slight twitch to his lips. "I did notice that part. I assume we'll be spending time in there after the coffee?"

"You would assume right, big guy." She patted his arm, then had to force her hand away when she got distracted by the feel of him. Her sexy as hell leopard shifter mate was almost as addictive as coffee and their mate bond ensured she could not get enough of him. Fortunately, this was not a hardship in her life.

Other things in her life were complicated and a pain in the ass. Deacon was not one of those things.

The coffee shop had at least a dozen people scattered around the round wooden tables, in various states of typical café activities. Two different people on laptops, mugs beside them as they focused on whatever was happening on their screens. A trio of teenagers all talking while also scrolling their phones, which Cary found impressive because the conversation seemed to be about who was the best philosopher, Jung or Canto. Although, she might have been hearing that wrong and they could be talking about sports people or musical people or fellow students. Hard to say with her ordinary human hearing. Deacon probably knew with his super shifter hearing.

There was an older woman sitting in the very middle of the café sipping on a mug and reading an erotic novel with a very racy cover—Cary would have to remember that cover and look into that book later. A woman with a baby stroller cooing at the baby inside while she downed a very large coffee. A man reading a book Cary couldn't see as he sipped his drink and occasionally glanced up at the barista. And a couple of people who liked like they might work nearby and were here on a break—she was pretty sure it was a weekday. Maybe?

Hard to remember. Her job was a kind of twenty-four hour on call thing so she didn't pay attention to weekdays and weekends. And Deacon had taken a few days off because his twin sister was in town and there was definitely something going on there but no one had deigned to tell her about it yet and wasn't that a state of affairs she intended to do something about.

Despite the crowd, there were still a few free tables. And she'd been on her feet for long enough she wanted a seat. Plus the call of the coffee was drawing her toward the counter. So coffee first. Then off to bookshop because she was nosey and she wanted to know if that book the older woman was reading was any good.

Deacon set a hand to her lower back as they headed toward the counter and the awaiting barista and this gave Cary a warm, melty feeling all over. She still couldn't believe he could do that to her with such a simple touch. The man was truly a wonder. She was delighted he'd turned out to be her wonder, though.

At the long wooden counter, the barista waited, smiling at them. "What can I get you?"

Cary was so tempted to say, "I'll have what she's having" about the woman reading the erotic book. So. Tempted. Her obsession with 80s music and movies was a source of much amusement to her family and a shared obsession with her friend Marianne. Deacon, who'd been an actual adult in the eighties—because shifters aged differently and even though he looked in his mid-thirties, and was about that "age" in leopard shifter years, he had actually passed fifty-eight years on the planet—did not understand her all-things-80s obsession but he did indulge it. For which she was grateful.

The barista looked young enough, though, she probably

wouldn't get the reference. Though her age was difficult to judge—and Cary sucked at judging ages anyway since her job required her to be around preternatural and supernatural beings (like her mate) who either didn't age or aged differently to humans—the barista looked like she was probably in her late twenties-early thirties. Which, though Cary was only in her early thirties—because you weren't mid-thirties until you hit thirty-five and that was a hill she would die on—most people her age, outside of Marianne and Lucy (Angie was that little bit older so she didn't count in this and had a valid reason for her enjoyment of all things 80s), did not know 80s references.

A long way to get to the fact that she didn't, despite much desire, spout the line and just grinned. "Largest coffee you have available. Milk and sweetener are excellent. This place is adorable."

The barista grinned. "Thank you for that. I've worked really hard to ensure it's comfortable for people."

"You have accomplished that. Though how could you go wrong opening a coffee shop attached to a bookstore."

"Exactly!" The barista looked at the very large Maine coon cat sprawled over the top of a stool that looked entirely too small for the little beastie. "Told you so," she said to the cat.

The cat, for his part, licked a paw and gave Deacon a very long stare.

Occasionally, cats took issue with the large human who smelled like cat. Not always. Dogs were more of an issue for Deacon, though her little three dog pack had accepted him right away. But since Deacon's job was rescuing animals—and wasn't *that* just amazing and made him even more perfect for Cary—he always found a way to deal with the animals that might have problems with large cats walking in their midst. It was a family business so all his leopard shifter siblings were good at that. His twin brother was even a vet!

The Maine coon and Deacon spent a few moments staring at each other, the cat gave Deacon a sort of nod, Deacon nodded back, and they both went back to what they'd been doing. Deacon checking the menu behind the counter and the Maine coon licking his paws.

"That's Boo," the barista/café owner said. "Ignore him. He's got an attitude."

Cary would swear she heard the cat release a short, sharp hiss before purring so loudly he sounded like an engine gearing up.

She chuckled. "I love all animals, his attitude is perfect."

The café owner grinned. "Can I get you anything else besides the one coffee?"

Deacon frowned a little. "I don't suppose I could get a glass of milk. Just milk."

The café owner paused only a beat before saying, "Skim or whole? With or without ice?"

"No ice. Whole."

Cary reached back and took his hand. Her big cat shifter drinking milk always made her grin. The fact that it had barely fazed the café owner was a testament to her professionalism.

The woman rang up their order and said, "Make

yourselves comfortable. I'll bring this over to you in just a minute."

Cary and Deacon found a table near one wall of the café, a position that allowed her to see the door and all the people coming and going. Part of that was a habit from her job—she didn't *have* to see bad guys coming but it helped—and part was because she was nosey and wanted to watch all the people coming and going. It also gave her a good view into the bookstore where she intended on spending some time after getting a much-needed caffeine boost.

"So," she said to Deacon as they waited, "are you going to tell me what's happening with Jocelyn or is it private and you can't talk about it?"

He pulled in a deep breath, let it out slowly. "As my mate, I would tell you anything. I do tell you everything. That I can."

"But this is Jocelyn's private life and not yours to tell." Cary nodded and let out a sigh. "I figured. But I'm curious so I thought I'd ask."

"If and when she gives me permission to discuss it, I'll fill you in." He took her hand across the table, gently circling his thumb over her fingers.

She got distracted by the gesture for a beat before saying, "It's fine. Really. I don't want to violate her privacy." But yeah, no, she was super curious and that wasn't going away any time soon. If he *could* explain it all one day, she would be all in, popcorn in lap, ready to listen.

The barista brought her coffee and Deacon's milk a minute later, giving them a friendly smile before heading back to the counter. On the way, she glanced at the man sitting alone in a cushioned chair by the front window—the man Cary had noticed glanced at the barista regularly. The barista looked away quickly and an adorable blush rose up her cheeks. Cary grinned.

Well, she might not get the gossip on Deacon's sister, but she could content herself with imagining all the stories going on inside the café. Starting with the man by the window and the café owner.

Her fist sip of coffee left her humming under her breath, a deep sigh of satisfaction.

Deacon grinned at her. "All better now?"

"Superb." She grinned back.

Or at least she was happy until the door to the café opened and that warning tingling along her back started up.

The warning that her particular brand of help was needed.

⁂

The man who stepped into the café didn't look threatening outwardly. That happened sometimes. Bad guys just looked like ordinary people, walking around, doing life without anyone noticing they were dangerous and not nice. Cary wasn't even sure she would have realized this guy was bad news if it weren't for her Protector instincts kicking in.

Being a magical Protector was ever so slightly like being a superhero—at least that's what she liked to think—and meant she had these skills. But instead of instincts born of a radioactive spider bite, she had Protector instincts. And instead of a secret cave with all her cool stuff in it, she had a secret attic with all her cool stuff in it. Although her cool stuff included a lot of very weird books she wouldn't want her mother to see and a computer linked up to the parts of the internet she wouldn't be able to access on her ordinary laptop —she had someone who'd set that up for her, she wouldn't know how to access a dark net if it fell over her head.

At any rate, what Cary did know was how to protect people from bad guys. It was her entire job. She even got paid for it. She channeled magic given to her by her bosses—the North American Fae who created Protectors—and that magic created a lovely shield and that lovely shield kept all the bad guys out and all the good guys in. Cary just had to be between them.

She often described herself as a walking, talking Kevlar vest. This was an accurate description. She could even stop bullets with her shield—though not always in time to keep from getting a bruise, but that was another story.

The trick really was to get between the good guy and bad guy in time—and a burst of more-than-human speed was within her realm of the possible thanks to the Protector magic —but that was even trickier when you weren't sure who the good guy was. And in this case, while Cary was quite certain the man who just walked in was the "bad guy" she could not for the life of her figure out who the "good guy" was because the man who'd just entered didn't look around the place like he was looking for someone. He didn't hone in on one person. He gave the café a cursory glance, the way Cary had when she'd entered, and then went right to the counter to order a coffee.

Cary did notice that the café owner looked a little more stiff and formal with the new customer. But she didn't look in obvious distress, and the man only gave the owner enough attention to place and pay for his order. Most of his attention appeared to be turned inward.

He wasn't the one Cary was supposed to be protecting. She could feel that. He was the threat. But she couldn't tell who he was threatening. And that made it very difficult to get between him and the someone. Keeping one eye on the man, she glanced around at the other patrons to see if anyone was looking at him too.

Deacon of course had gone quiet the minute she straightened in her seat and muttered, "Shit." He knew what that meant. Knew the look she got when she had to go save someone. He held himself perfectly still, waiting for her to move, his gaze also tracking around the café. There was a very very faint hint of yellow in his golden eyes, just the barest sign of his leopard raising its head. But he seemed well controlled—probably because there was no immediate threat to *her*—so she didn't worry about him.

Everyone else in the café seemed to still be doing their own thing. The three teenagers had left for the bookstore, and a couple of other people had wandered in from the bookstore. The man by the window who'd been exchanging looks with the café owner was watching her, his mouth turned down slightly, his attention more obvious now. Watchful, but in that way that actually reminded Cary of

Deacon. A sort of waiting-to-act coiled sort or watchfulness.

Waiting to see if the owner needed help.

That was interesting all on its own, and if she didn't need to get to work soon, she'd have watched that like a TV show. But it was obvious he wasn't the one in danger here. And it didn't seem to be the café owner either.

The man in the back of the café pounding away at his computer was still pounding away. The woman who'd been working on hers had since closed her laptop and was sipping her coffee while flipping through a magazine.

No one looked in distress or panicky. No one but the man at the window, the owner of the café, and Cary and Deacon were paying the newcomer any attention.

What the hell?

Her instincts were screaming at her to move, to get between that man and…someone. But which someone?

She couldn't remember ever having this problem before. The good guy was almost always obvious. Mostly because the bad guy was already proving they were the bad guy by going after the good guy by the time Cary's instincts started up. She'd rarely encountered someone her instincts screamed was the threat without having someone also standing right there being threatened.

This was weird. "This is weird," she murmured to Deacon.

"What's happening?" He leaned across the table and took her hand, pretending at casual even though his muscles were all tense and ready for action.

Again, under different circumstances, she'd have indulged in admiring those coiled muscles. "I'm not sure." She leaned forward to whisper too. But in her case, she didn't have to worry that he'd hear her. She could whisper at him from across the room and he'd hear her. "The man who just walked in triggered my Protector instincts in a bad way. I need to get between him and someone. But the someone isn't presenting themselves so I'm not sure what to do."

"The owner doesn't like him," Deacon murmured.

"No she does not. Her admirer is ready to jump to her rescue as well. But no one else in here seems to be paying any attention to the man."

"You know you're supposed to protect someone from him and not, say, protect him from someone?"

She shook her head just a little. "He's the bad guy. Certain of it. Just…" She scowled and glanced around. "No idea who the good guy is."

"This is weird."

"Very." She scanned the café again. Maybe it was someone due to walk in soon?

She kind of wanted to ask the owner if that man came in regularly. The owner might have been formal with him because he was a regular that she knew was bad news? But Cary wasn't sure how to broach that topic without it being weird. She couldn't very well explain that she needed to get between him and someone he intended on hurting but she wasn't sure who that someone was. And also she didn't tell people she was a Protector. The less people knew about her and what she did, and most importantly *how* she did it, the safer for everyone.

Several tense moments passed without anything happening. And then a middle-aged man carrying a small, fluffy dog walked into the café from the bookstore. He was maybe Cary's height, which was a little shorter than average for a man, with dark hair liberally sprinkled with gray. He wore a colorful pair of pink and orange pants with a geometric pattern in blue on them, a plain white cotton t-shirt, and a blue kerchief tied around his neck like a cravat. Half his face was clean shaven, the other half had a full beard and mustache—and she imagined that took a lot of effort to maintain such a precise line down the middle of his mouth and chin. And he wore a bowler hat on his head at a jaunty angle.

He was a study in contrasts. Designed to stick out in a crowd. Eccentric. But in that sort of pleasant way that Cary admired in people. Being his true self. She loved that.

He cooed at the dog in his arms as they moved into the café, the dog's tail wagging, its little tongue hanging out. "Maybe they'll have a biscuit for you," the man said, his voice surprisingly deep—though she wasn't sure why that surprised her. "Would you like a biscuit, Betty?"

A dog named Betty.

Perfect.

"You suppose his name is Al?" Deacon whispered.

"Huh?"

"Nothing." Deacon smiled at her briefly. Then grew serious again. "That's your good guy, isn't it?"

"He is," she said and patted Deacon's hands. "I'll be back."

She stood and, as casually as she could manage, she set herself between the man in the bowler hat and his dog Betty, and the man she knew was a threat. She made a sort of pretense at walking toward the counter as if she intended on ordering something else but really was just positioning herself to protect Betty and her owner.

Which was good timing because that's when the man she'd been certain was a bad guy stood up from the seat he'd taken and started toward Betty and her owner.

Drawing a knife as he charged.

———

Cary heard all the exclamations around her, the gasps, the curse from the owner. She heard the man behind her let out a surprised squeak and Betty started barking—the little dog had a very high-pitched bark. The man with the knife over his head charged Betty's owner.

And Cary took a single step to the side. Placing her right in between the knife guy and the dog guy.

This resulted in the knife bouncing off her shield in an almost comic way that sent the attacker backward a step.

Silence and stillness reigned for a full twenty seconds after that.

Cary could see from the corner of her eye that the café owner had come out from behind the counter, her admirer was now standing, and strangely—or not so strangely—the Maine coon cat was now inching toward the man with the knife.

She looked directly at the cat and said, "Don't get hurt. I've got this. You can go back to napping."

The cat stilled, looked at her in that slow way that proved Cary's guess had been right, and then he licked his lips, blinked his pale blue eyes, turned and leapt back up onto his too small stool, circling a few times before sprawling across it again. The cat did keep his attention on the happenings, but he stayed out of the way.

This was good. Cary would absolutely have to jump in and save him if he got into trouble because Cary *always* protected animals. But that could get complicated in this situation. Better to have the bad guy focused on only one person and that person was already under Cary's protection.

"So," she said into the still ringing silence that followed her comment to the cat, "what's all this about then?"

"He stole my dog," the man with the knife said. "She's worth a fortune. I want her back."

Since said dog was behind Cary growling low in her throat in an almost subsonic show of "no," Cary was going to assume Betty was happier with the man with the bright pants and jaunty hat.

"She was never *your* dog," the man behind her said. "She was *our* dog and you gave up any rights to her when you tried to sell her off to a breeder."

Yeah, that didn't sound nice.

But it also sounded like some really interesting gossip

and Cary was up for listening to the gossip now she was sure no one would get hurt.

"She could have gotten me out of debt and all you cared about was keeping her to yourself," the man with the knife snarled.

"Do you know what they would have done to her at the breeders!" shouted Betty's owner—yes, Cary saw the man behind her as the sole owner of Betty now. She knew what went on at some breeders. She'd been a vet tech before her job change to Protector.

"Do you understand what they'll do to me if I don't pay them back?" the knifeman hissed, getting as close to them as Cary's shield would allow, then scowling at the empty air that refused to let him pass.

From her right, Cary could just hear the owner speaking to someone quietly on the phone, probably a 911 operator. Cary didn't tend to like when the cops showed up because they complicated things and sometimes gave her more people to protect, depending on the situation. Also, they asked questions she couldn't answer, like, "How could you just stand there and not get stabbed when that man had a knife he kept trying to stab you with?"

That was a complicated question to answer when you didn't want to tell the truth because it might get you locked up but also couldn't tell the truth because it was dangerous for you.

But in this case, with all these witnesses, it would be weird if no one did call the cops, and even weirder if there were no cops arriving to take care of the man with the knife.

Maybe Cary could just…slip out after they arrived. She'd miss her bookstore shopping spree, but she could always come back. Outside of the knife-wielding bad guy, she really liked this café.

Until the cops arrived, though, Cary needed to keep the knife-wielding bad guy talking. If he left that would be fine, too, but it would make it harder for the cops to arrest him.

"Who do you have to pay back and why and how much?" There was just no way he was going to answer those questions.

"I'm not telling you anything, you bitch. Get out of my way."

She told herself so. No way he'd answer. She was not counting on the man behind her with Betty telling her everything, however.

"He bets," Betty's owner said. "He throws all his money into a gambling addiction. And anything Betty ever earned on the dog show circuit he also gambled away. We broke up because he couldn't stop throwing good money after bad with increasingly dangerous bets."

"I just need one more chance. The next one will pay off. But I can't make that bet without up-front money. And I can't get up-front money without that fucking dog."

Cary moved a little more firmly in front of Betty and her owner. She realized she might actually be protecting the dog more than the man but that was just as well. She always protected animals.

"Betty isn't your bargaining chip or yours to sell off," Betty's owner said. "And she's not getting sent off to some puppy mill to pop out endless rounds of babies after they've breed her with unacceptable males."

The disgust in his voice echoed Cary's sentiments.

"You don't understand," the man with the knife said. "They will *kill* me. I need to give them something."

"That's your own problem. You shouldn't have gotten in with them in the first place."

"They?" Cary asked over her shoulder, though she already knew. It was always one of two kinds of people and either kind were quick to take out a man's knees if they didn't get their money back.

"Loan sharks," Betty's owner said.

Yup. Definitely one of the two potentials. "They'll probably only take your knees," she told the knife man. "Those types want their money back and they can't get money from a dead man."

The man with the knife wiped the back of his hand across his mouth, then charged at her with the knife raised.

She scowled and shook her head as he bounced off her shield. "That was ridiculous. Stop. You're embarrassing yourself."

From behind her, she was pretty sure she heard Deacon growl. But he was safely behind her, under her protection if he needed it, and she was between him and the guy with the knife so the guy with the knife was safe from Deacon. She really really hated protecting bad guys, especially from the man she loved, but what could she do. It was her job.

The knife man waved his knife at her. "How are you doing that?"

"Just a knack. You know they've called the cops, right?"

He looked around more frantically now. "The cops will turn me over to them. They'll kill me."

She wasn't sure *that* was true.

Although, she wasn't sure it wasn't true either.

"In that case," she said pragmatically, "maybe you should run away."

"Not without that fucking dog." He lunged again, so hard he bounced off her shield and landed on his ass on the ground.

She sighed and shook her head. "Embarrassing."

"I will gut you," the man screamed from the floor.

"Your dumb ass is laid out flat on the ground. How do you propose to do that?" She was losing patience for this guy. Especially since he was trying to use poor Betty to save himself from a mess he'd created for himself. "Get therapy. Join a twelve-step program. Get help. Do something that isn't horrible for once."

Knife guy shoved himself back to his feet. But he'd managed to drop his knife. He swung around, hunting for it.

He and Cary realized at the same time the knife had slid over the floor to the man by the window who'd been making eyes at the café owner. The man was standing and he had his foot on the knife. Knife Man would have to shove him over to get at his weapon again. Window Man did not look like the kind of person who would be easy to shove over. Which kind of surprised Cary because he'd looked perfectly innocuous when sitting at the window.

Huh. Interesting.

Also, though, how had the knife even gotten that far away? Cary hadn't heard it slid. And she hadn't thought Knife Man had hit the ground hard enough for that to send the knife so far. But maybe she'd been distracted by Knife Man's pathetic plan.

"There you have it," she said. "No more knife. You're not getting Betty. And the police should be here any minute. Run away. Get therapy. Get into a program. Do better. Maybe you'll survive."

"Bitch," Knife Man yelled as he charged her again. She shook her head. This really was ridiculous.

Window Man made to move toward her but she raised a hand and shook her head as Knife Man bounced off her shield. Again. This hit sent him flying back against the café door. Cary winced since the door was glass, but fortunately it didn't break.

"What are you doing to him?" Betty's owner whispered —not very quietly—to Cary.

"He's doing this to himself," she said. A sort of hand wavy way of avoiding a proper answer. But, technically, also true. If he'd stop charging her shield, he'd stop getting thrown around.

From down the street, she could just hear the approach of sirens. Knife Man must have heard the sound at the same time because his eyes widened and he fumbled his way out of the café. She watched him look both ways on the street, before running off in the opposite direction from the sirens.

"You suppose he'll get into a program for his addiction?" she asked Betty's owner over her shoulder.

"No. I tried that tact for the last two years. He's hopeless." Cary turned to see Betty's owner scratching Betty under the chin. "And he was trying to hurt you, wasn't he?" he said in a cooing voice. "But daddy won't let anyone hurt his baby."

Betty's little fluffy tail wagged furiously as she licked the man's face—the side that was shaven.

Window Man joined them at the same time as the café owner came around the counter.

"Everyone okay?" she asked the other customers.

There was a series of muttered affirmatives and relieved sighs.

"A coffee on the house for everyone," the owner said. To Cary, she added, "You can have free coffee for life."

Cary waved that way—even though it was tempting. "That's not necessary. But I will take one of the free ones now." She got paid for her job, but it was still nice to receive the occasional small gesture of gratitude. When that gratitude came in the form of coffee. Or books. But they weren't in that half of the store, so…

"The knife is under the table, when the cops get here," Window Man said to the café owner. "You're okay?"

She smiled at him and nodded.

Cary grinned and rocked back on her heels, watching them. She loved a good budding romance. And it looked like these two were in the early stages. How sweet.

Deacon came up behind her and set a hand to hear shoulder. She sighed. Speaking of romance.

"You okay?" he murmured close to her ear.

"Of course. But thanks for asking. Also, thanks for not attacking that man when he kept threatening us."

"I've learned not to do that," Deacon said, sounding offended. "But…" And now he sounded a little embarrassed. "It was more the way he was talking about Betty. I hate puppy mills."

She turned and gave him a big smacking kiss right on the mouth. This was exactly why she loved him so much.

"I'm afraid the police will probably need your statement," the café owner said to Betty's owner. "Coffee and pastry to make the wait more bearable?"

"Yes, please," the man said. "Black coffee. And one of those croissants you get. They're delicious."

"You got it."

Before the owner walked away, though, she turned to Cary. "I should probably get your name after you stopped a potentially horrible situation.

Cary grinned. "Cary. It's nice to meet you."

"Nina. This is my place. And you're always welcome. I'm sure I can get the bookstore owner to extend you a discount too, if you like books."

"I love books." She was going to have a hard time saying no to that discount, so she might not. She had a bunch of new hardbacks she'd been looking to buy. "And it was nothing."

Nina snort-laughed. "I swear we do not get knife-wielding men in here every day, so it was handy you happened to be here."

"Definitely." Though, given her job, Cary sort of suspected it was more than a coincidence. She always seemed to land where Trouble was about to happen. Hazards of the job, she supposed.

Nina headed back to the counter and Window Guy followed, giving the cat on the stool a little head scratch as he stopped at the counter to speak quietly with Nina.

Cary gave that cat a look. The cat looked back. Yeah, she was pretty positive he was a familiar. But probably best not to discuss that with Nina while the café was so full. She hadn't met a proper witch familiar in person before, even though one of her best friends was a witch. Cary was very curious how that all worked.

Questions for later.

She turned to Betty's owner. "I should get your name too."

"Al," he said with a grin.

"Told you," Deacon said.

"I still don't get the joke." She looked between the two men who were smiling at each other.

"It's from a Paul Simon song," Al said.

"Ah." Now she remembered it. And was embarrassed she hadn't before. Her obsession with all things 80s had let her down.

Because she was embarrassed, she changed the subject. "If you don't mind my asking, what was the thinking behind the half beard, half clean-shaven look? I'm not sure I've ever seen that particular style of facial hair before." She kind of liked it. It was so precise and interesting.

Al chuckled. "I'm in a play. It's very avant-garde. Very experimental. I play two different roles at the same time and the director wanted the two characters to have different looks." He gestured at his face. "Thus the facial hair."

"Cool." Cary got the information for his play, fully intending on going to see it.

Al went to get his coffee when Nina called him over. And Cary leaned back into Deacon. "You sure you want to stay and talk to the cops," he murmured next to her ear.

"I would rather not. But I have a feeling Nina can handle the more…mysterious aspects of what just happened."

"Because she's a witch with a familiar and so not unaccustomed to dealing with paranormal things?"

Cary chuckled. "Wondered if you'd spotted that."

"Her familiar won't talk to me, but there were some subsonic growls while we established the boundaries of me being here."

"Really? Cool. I didn't know you could do that." And that gave her a whole bunch of questions to ask her mate.

But after coffee. And maybe after some book shopping.

A police car pulled up outside, and Nina dealt with the two officers who walked into the café like a pro. The man who'd been pounding away at his computer went back to furiously pounding the keyboard until the cops asked for his statement. The rest of the people in the café gave their statements then settled back in with their free drinks. No one seemed particularly bothered by the interlude with a knife-wielding man.

Even the cops settled at the counter for a couple of coffees and some croissants, completely ignoring Cary and Deacon.

The fact that they didn't have to answer questions or give a statement and no one in the café seemed to notice was something that did *not* go unnoticed to Cary. She gave Nina a raised eyebrow.

Nina gave her a wink.

Cary grinned.

Yeah. She was definitely coming back to this café.

MAGIC MYSTERY ROMANCE

STORYTIME at The Cafe

KATSIMONSBOOKS

Mystery

URBAN FANTASY

Romance

And More!

KATSIMONSBOOKS.COM

The CARY REDMOND Series

GOT TROUBLE?

Don't Miss a Single Book in this
Action-Packed Romantic Urban Fantasy Series

The Dragon Thief Series

Don't Miss this Action-Packed
Urban Fantasy Romance Series

JOIN KAT'S NEWSLETTER

STAY UP-TO-DATE

On all Kat's News, Updates, and fun extras

New Subscriber Get Two Exclusive Stories Just for Signing up!

bit.ly/KatSimonsNewsletter

BOOKS BY KAT SIMONS

STORIES FROM THE CAFE

VOLUME ONE

Boo and the Witch

Henry

Agnes

Frank

Betty and Al

Carrie Ann

Joan of Kerry

Myra and Christopher

Jamar

Nina and Boo and Rhys Witherby Too

Sam and Becky

Kassidey

Cary and Deacon

ALSO BY KAT SIMONS

Paranormal Romance

Seven Families: Wolf Series

Dragon Thief Series

Tiger Shifters Series

Romancing the Leopard: A Tiger Shifters-Cary Redmond Crossover Novel

Destiny Cats Series

Urban Fantasy

The Cary Redmond Series

Cary Redmond Short Stories and Collections

Demon Witch Series

Joan of Kerry Series

Friday's Curious Shop Series

Contemporary Fantasy

Haunts and Howls Collections

**Tombstone Wizard * The Unshattered Sword * Going Out of Business: Everything's for Sale * Anger Management * Demonic Dates * The Museum of Small Art's Everyman * Burning Inside a Stone Circle * Bored Questless * I Just Ate a Bug * Ting Ling * Sophie Saves the World * Black Water Hawthorns * To Dance in Fallow Fields at Midnight * The Troll and the Dressmaker **

Mystery and Thriller

Ross and O'Neill Adventures

Galileo's Pendulum

Percy James Mysteries

Movies May Murder

Cookies Can't Crime

Diamonds Do Damage

Replicas Risk Ruin

Vacation Deadly: An Action Adventure Thriller Collection

Pick Your Genre Collections

Who Steals a Dragon

Contemporary Romances

Designed for You

Poinsettias and Possibilities

ABOUT THE AUTHOR

Bestselling, award-winning author Kat Simons earned her Ph.D. in animal behavior, working with animals as diverse as dolphins and deer. She brought her experience and knowledge of biology to her paranormal romance and urban fantasy fiction, where she delights in taking nature and turning it on its ear. She writes urban fantasy, contemporary fantasy, and paranormal romance in series which combine action adventure, the otherworldly, and a frequent dose of sexy romance.

After spending many years writing primarily paranormal and urban fantasy romances, in 2022 Kat also debuts in contemporary romance with the release of her first contemporary romance novel, DESIGNED FOR YOU. First, but not the last, because Kat loves writing trope-tastic romance fun with heartwarming Happily Ever Afters.

In 2022 Kat also releases her first action-adventure thriller, GALILEO'S PENDULUM, which brings a mix of science history and fast-paced adventure to a little light forgery as her heroes race around the world to save an ancient relic. She also writes a soft-boiled, amateur sleuth series set in New York City, the Percy James series, about the adventures and exploits of front a desk receptionist working in a boutique hotel on the Upper East Side of Manhattan. Percy James sees a lot in that small hotel. And not all of it is legal.

Kat also publishes fantasy, science fiction, and the occasional hockey romance under the name Isabo Kelly (https://www.isabokelly.com), because of course she does.

After traveling the world, living in places like Hawaii, Germany, and Ireland, Kat now lives in New York City with her family and a library's worth of books.

For more on Kat and her future books
You can find her at

KatSimonsBooks
https://www.katsimonsbooks.com
https://www.TheCafeatKatSimonsBooks.com

Or look for her at

Website: https://www.katsimons.com/
Newsletter: https://bit.ly/KatSimonsNewsletter

Social Media
Facebook Page: https://www.facebook.com/
KatSimonsAuthor
BookBub: https://www.bookbub.com/authors/kat-simons
Instagram: https://www.instagram.com/isabokelly/
Threads: https://www.threads.net/@isabokelly
Bluesky: https://bsky.app/profile/katsimons.bsky.social